At Harlequin Presents we are always interested in what you, the readers, think about the series. So if you have any thoughts you'd like to share, please join in the discussion of your favorite books at www.iheartpresents.com—created by and for fans of Harlequin Presents!

On the site, find blog entries written by authors and fans, the inside scoop from editors and links to authors and books. Enjoy and share with others the unique world of Presents— we'd love to hear from you!

DESERT KINGS

*Blood brothers, hot-blooded lovers—
who will they take as their queens?*
These Arabian brothers stand majestically on a
desert horizon, silhouetted against sand dunes
by the white-hot sun. The sheikhs are blood
brothers, rulers of all they survey. But though
used to impossible wealth and luxury, they also
thrive on the barbaric beauty of their kingdom.
Are there women with spirit enough to tame
these hard, proud kings and become their
lifelong queens?

Available this month:

The Sheikh's Chosen Queen

Coming next month:

King of the Desert, Captive Bride
Sheikh Khalid Fehr may be the youngest
of the royal brothers, but it makes him no less
passionate and powerful—he lives and breathes
for the desert. He'll give his darkened soul to the
woman who captures it!

Look on Jane's Web site for more about the
Desert Kings!

Jane Porter

THE SHEIKH'S CHOSEN QUEEN

DESERT KINGS

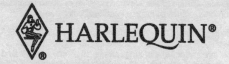
HARLEQUIN®

TORONTO • NEW YORK • LONDON
AMSTERDAM • PARIS • SYDNEY • HAMBURG
STOCKHOLM • ATHENS • TOKYO • MILAN • MADRID
PRAGUE • WARSAW • BUDAPEST • AUCKLAND

ISBN-13: 978-0-373-12717-7
ISBN-10:   0-373-12717-0

THE SHEIKH'S CHOSEN QUEEN

First North American Publication 2008.

www.eHarlequin.com

Printed in U.S.A.

All about the author...
Jane Porter

Born in Visalia, California, I'm a small-town girl at heart. As a little girl I spent hours on my bed, staring out the window, dreaming of far-off places, fearless knights and happy-ever-after endings. In my imagination I was never the geeky bookworm with the thick Coke-bottle glasses, but a princess, a magical fairy, a Joan-of-Arc crusader.

My parents fed my imagination by taking our family to Europe for a year when I was thirteen. The year away changed me, and overseas I discovered a huge and wonderful world with different cultures and customs. I loved everything about Europe, but felt especially passionate about Italy and those gorgeous Italian men (no wonder my very first Presents hero was Italian).

I confess, after that incredible year in Europe, the travel bug bit, and I spent much of my school years abroad, studying in South Africa, Japan and Ireland.

After my years of traveling and studying I had to settle down and earn a living. With my bachelor's degree from UCLA in American studies, a program that combines American literature and American history, I've worked in sales and marketing, and have been a director of a nonprofit foundation. Later I earned my master's in writing from the University of San Francisco, and taught junior and high school English.

I now live in rugged Seattle, Washington, with my two young sons. I never mind a rainy day, either, because that's when I sit at my desk and write stories about faraway places, fascinating people and, most importantly of all, love.

I love to hear from my readers. You can write to me at P.O. Box 524, Bellevue, WA 98009, USA.

For my mother-in-law, Jackie Gaskins.
God has a new and feisty angel in heaven.

PROLOGUE

HOW DID A king ask for a favor?

In the palace courtyard, King Sharif Fehr broke the rosebud off the stem and held the half-opened bud in his palm, the blush petals almost pink against his skin. Roses were difficult to grow in his country's desert heat, which only made them more rare and beautiful.

So how did a king ask for help?

How did a king get what he needed?

Carefully, he answered himself, his thumb stroking a tender petal. Very carefully.

CHAPTER ONE

THE LOW heels on Jesslyn Heaton's practical navy pumps clicked briskly against the sidewalk as she left the administrative office.

It was the last day of school and mercifully the students had finally been sent home stuffed full of cupcakes and gallons of shocking red punch. All she had to do now was close her room for the summer.

"Going anywhere fun for holiday, Miss Heaton?" a student asked, his thin, reedy voice breaking on her name.

Jesslyn glanced up from the paperwork she'd pulled from her faculty mailbox. "Aaron, you haven't left yet? School ended hours ago."

The freckle-faced teen blushed. "Forgot something," he mumbled, his flush deepening as he reached into his backpack to retrieve a small package wrapped in white paper and tied with a purple silk ribbon. "For you. My mom picked it out. But it was my idea."

"A present." Jesslyn smiled and adjusted the pile of paperwork in her arms to take the gift. "That's so thoughtful. But Aaron, it's not necessary. I'll see you next school term—"

"I won't be back." His shoulders rose and he hunched miserably into the backpack he'd slung again onto his thin back.

"We're moving this summer. Dad's been transferred back to the States. Anchorage, I think."

Having taught middle school at the small private school in the United Arab Emirates for the past six years, Jesslyn had witnessed how abruptly the students—children of ex-pats—came and went. "I'm sorry, Aaron. I really am."

He shoved his hands deeper into his pockets. "Maybe you could tell the other kids? Have them e-mail me?"

His voice cracked again, and it was the crack in his voice along with the way he hung his head that nearly undid her. These children went through so much. Foreign homes, foreign lives, change the only constant. "I will, of course."

Nodding, he turned around and was gone, rushing down the empty corridors of the school. Jesslyn watched his hasty departure for a moment before unlocking the door to her deserted classroom with a sigh. Hard to believe that another school year had ended. It seemed like only yesterday she was handing out the mountain of textbooks and carefully printing children's names in her class register. Now they were gone, and for the next two months she was free.

Well, she'd be free as soon as she closed up her classroom, and she couldn't do that until she tackled her last, and least-favorite task, washing the chalkboards.

Twenty minutes later her once-crisp navy dress stuck to the small of her back, and perspiration matted the heavy dark hair at her nape. What a job, she thought, wrinkling her nose as she rinsed out the filthy sponge in the sink.

A knock sounded on her door and Dr. Maddox, her principal, appeared in the doorway. "Miss Heaton, you've a guest."

Jesslyn thought one of her students' parents had shown up, concerned about a grade on a report, but it wasn't Robert.

Heart suddenly racing, she stared stunned at Sharif Fehr. *Prince* Sharif Fehr.

She convulsively squeezed the wet sponge, water streaming through her now-trembling fingers.

Sharif.

Sharif, here?

Impossible. But he was here, it was without a doubt Prince Fehr standing in her doorway, tall, imposing, real. She stared at him, drinking him in, adrenaline racing through her veins, too hot, too cold, too intense.

Dr. Maddox cleared her throat. "Miss Heaton, it is my pleasure to introduce you to our most generous school benefactor, His Royal Highness—"

"Sharif," Jesslyn whispered, unable to stop herself.

"Jesslyn," Sharif answered with a slight nod.

And just like that, her name spoken in his rich, deep voice made the years disappear.

The last time she'd seen him they'd been younger, so much younger. She'd been a young woman in her first year of teaching at the American School in London. And he'd been a gorgeous, rebel Arab prince who wore jeans and flip-flops and baggy cashmere sweatshirts.

Now he looked like someone altogether different. His baggy sweatshirts were gone, and the faded, torn jeans were replaced by a *dishdashah* or a *thoub*, as more commonly known in the Arabian Gulf, a cool, long, one-piece white dress and the traditional head gear comprised of a *gutrah*, a white scarflike cloth, and the *ogal*, the black circular band that held everything together.

He looked so different from when she'd last seen him, and yet he still looked very much the same, from the piercing pewter eyes to his chiseled jaw to his dark, glossy hair.

Confused, Dr. Maddox glanced from one to the other. "You know each other?"

Know? *Know?* She'd been his, and he'd been hers and their lives had been so intertwined that ending their relationship had ripped her heart to shreds.

"We...we went to school together," she stammered, cheeks heating as she unsuccessfully tried to avoid his eyes.

But his gaze found hers anyway and held, the corner of his mouth sardonically lifting, challenging her.

They didn't go to school together.

They weren't even enrolled in school at the same time. He had been six years older than her, and although he hadn't dressed the part, he had been a very successful financial analyst in London when they met.

They'd dated for several years, and when she broke it off, she walked away telling herself she would never see him again. And she hadn't.

That didn't mean she hadn't hoped he'd prove her wrong.

Finally he had. But why? What did he want? Because he did want something. Sharif Fehr wouldn't be in her Sharjah classroom without a very good reason.

"We went to school in England," she added, striving to sound blasé, trying to hide how deeply his surprise appearance had unnerved her. There were boyfriends in life from whom you parted on good terms and then there were the ones who had changed you forever.

Sharif had changed her forever, and now, despite all the years that had passed, just being in the same room with him made her nerves scream, Danger, danger, danger.

"What a small world," Dr. Maddox said, looking from one to the other.

"Indeed," Sharif answered with a slight inclination of his royal head.

Jesslyn squeezed the sponge even tighter, her pulse leaping as she wondered yet again what he was doing here. What did he want?

What could he want with her?

She was still a teacher. She still lived a simple, rather frugal life. She still wore her brown hair at her shoulders in virtually the same style she'd worn nine years ago. And unlike him, she hadn't ever married, although the man she'd been dating a couple of years ago had proposed. She hadn't accepted the proposal, though, knowing she didn't love him enough, not the way she'd loved Sharif.

But then, she'd never loved anybody the same way she'd loved Sharif.

Abruptly turning, she dropped the sponge in the sink, rinsed her hands and used one of the rough paper towels to dry them. "What can I do for you, Sharif?"

"I suppose I'm not needed here anymore," Dr. Maddox said with a sigh of disappointment. "I'll head back to my office. Good afternoon, Your Highness." And with a respectful nod of her head, she left them, gently closing the door behind her.

Jesslyn heard rather than saw her classroom door close, and she drew a quick painful breath realizing they were alone.

Alone with Sharif. After all these years.

"Sit, please," Sharif said, gesturing for her to sit down at her desk. "There's no reason for you to stand for me."

She glanced at her chair but didn't think her legs could carry her across a room, at least not quite yet. "Would you like a chair?" she asked instead.

"I'm fine," he answered.

"Then I'll stand, too."

His expression never changed. "I'd be more comfortable if you sat. *Please*."

It wasn't a request, though, it was a command, and Jesslyn looked at him, curious as well as surprised. He would never have used such an authoritative tone with her before. He'd never raised his voice or issued commands when she knew him. He'd always been gorgeous, confident, comfortable in his own skin. But he'd never been regal, never formal. He was both now.

Studying him more closely, she realized his face had changed more than she'd initially thought. His face was different. The years had subtly reshaped his features. His cheekbones were more pronounced, his jaw wider, stronger, his chin and brow also more defined.

Not a young man anymore but a man.

And not just any man but one of the most powerful leaders in the Middle East.

"Okay," she said, her voice suddenly husky, betraying her nervousness, "let me just clean up and I'll be happy to sit down."

Turning back to the sink, she quickly tucked the bucket and sponge beneath the sink, wiped the sink down with another paper towel and then threw it away.

"You have to wash the chalkboards yourself?" Sharif asked as she made her way to her desk, stepping carefully around a crate of athletic gear and a stack of books that still needed to be put away in the closet.

"We're responsible for our own boards."

"I would have thought the janitor would take care of that."

"We're always trying to save money," Jesslyn answered, kneeling down to pick up a misplaced paperback novel. She'd taught at this school, a small private school in Sharjah for four years now, and her classrooms were always warm, and downright sweltering in May, June and September.

Sharif's eyes narrowed. "Is that why it's a hundred degrees in here?"

She grimaced. So he'd noticed. "The air conditioner is on. Unfortunately, it doesn't seem to put out as much cool air as warm air." Taking a seat behind her desk, she prayed she looked more put together than she felt. "Is that why you're here? To make a list of our school's needs and then make a contribution?"

"If you help me, I'd be happy to make a contribution."

There it was, why he was here. He wanted her help. Jesslyn felt a heavy weight in her chest and realized she wasn't breathing.

Jesslyn forced herself to exhale and then inhale, trying to keep from dissolving into a state of panic. There was no reason to panic. She owed him nothing. Their relationship had ended nearly ten years ago.

Her attempt at cool, calm and collected ended when she caught sight of his expression. He was observing her intently, assessing her from head to toe.

Flushing, she shuffled papers nervously. "What kind of help do you need?"

"The kind you're good at." He was walking toward her, very slowly.

She tried to concentrate on what he was saying instead of his proximity, but he was coming too close, moving too quickly. "I'm a teacher, Sharif."

"Exactly." He stood over her, tall and imposing.

Had he always been this tall? "It's been a long time," she said.

"Nine years."

"Nine," she repeated, finding it nearly impossible to tear her gaze from his fiercely handsome features, features that had only grown harder and more beautiful over the years. The handsome prince had become a man. But then, he wasn't merely a prince anymore. He was Sarq's king.

With one hand she smoothed her skirt, feeling miserably dowdy, all too aware that her wardrobe and hairstyle were basic, practical, no nonsense. She'd never been a fashionista to start with, and nine years in the classroom had reduced both her wardrobe and her sense of style to nil.

She forced her lips into a professional smile. "After nine years, what could I possibly do to help you?"

"Teach," he answered simply.

She felt a funny flicker of emotion, an emotion that fell somewhere between unreasonable fury and tears. "That's right. I'm a teacher and you're a king."

Sharif's gray eyes held hers, his expression enigmatic. "You could have been my queen."

"You were never serious, Sharif."

A spark flared in his eyes, and explosive tension whipped the room. "Neither were you."

And just like that they were adversaries, on opposite sides of an insurmountable wall.

"Unfair and untrue," she said through gritted teeth, anger making her chest too hot and tight. "There was no room for me—" She broke off, unable and unwilling to continue. It was history, so long ago it shouldn't matter. The fact that they were even discussing events of nine years ago struck her as tragic, especially as she had someone else in her life, someone who mattered a great deal to her. "So what *really* brings you here, King Fehr?"

His jaw hardened and his narrowed gaze ruthlessly swept her, head to toe. "I've told you. You do. I've come to offer you a job."

He was serious, then. This was about a job. *Teaching.*

Heat rushed through her, heat that left her deeply shaken.

Swallowing, she looked up at him, her smile so hard it felt brittle even to her. "I have a job."

"Apparently not a very good one," he answered, indicating the old chalkboards and battered room fixtures.

She wouldn't stoop to his level, wouldn't let herself be ridiculed, bullied or criticized. "It's one I like very much, thank you."

"Would you feel better if I told you the position is just for the summer?"

Her chin tilted even more defiantly. "No."

"Why not?"

It was on the tip of her tongue to tell him that she didn't have to answer to him, she didn't owe him anything. But that was a pointless exercise. It wasn't even the past holding her back, it was the future. She had plans for the summer, a wonderful eight and a half weeks of gorgeous, lovely travel—two weeks to beaches in Australia's Queensland, ski slopes in New Zealand, and lots of museum and theater excursions highlighted by great food in Sydney, Melbourne and Auckland. "Because…no."

"You'd be back here before school started in September," Sharif persisted, his tone so cool and smooth and relentless that goose bumps peppered her flesh.

"You remind me of my students when they're not listening."

He just smiled, grimly. "You haven't even considered the proposal."

"There's nothing to consider," she countered, amazed at his arrogance. "I've plans that can't be changed. Not even for you."

She saw his eyes narrow at her tone. She hadn't meant to be sarcastic, but there was a definite edge in her voice, an edge due to her discomfort. She didn't like the way he was towering over her desk, issuing dictates as though he were in his palace instead of her classroom, didn't like the way he pushed, didn't like his disregard for her, her feelings or her interests. "I appreciate you thinking of me, and I thank you for the invitation, King Fehr, but the answer is no."

"I'll pay you twice your salary—"

"Stop!" Her voice rang out as she slapped a heavy textbook down on her desk. The book thudded loudly, echoing in the classroom. "This isn't about money. I don't care about money. I don't care if you were to pay me two thousand dollars a day! I'm not interested. Not interested. Understand?"

Silence descended, a silence that felt positively deafening.

But it wasn't her fault she lost her temper, she reminded herself. He wasn't listening. "I'm going on holiday," she added, squaring her shoulders, refusing to be intimidated, even as her gaze clashed with his. Their relationship ended years ago, and there was no reason to start anything again— professionally or personally. "I leave tonight."

His features hardened, his expression so flinty his cheekbones and jaw looked as though they'd been chiseled from stone. "You can go on holiday next summer. I need you."

Jesslyn couldn't stifle a hysterical laugh. "You *need me?* Oh, that's a good one, King Fehr. Very funny indeed."

He wasn't laughing. His brows flattened over glittering gray eyes. "Give me one good reason why you won't even consider the position."

"I can give you three," she answered, impatiently stacking the teacher editions on her desk, one on top of the other. "I've just finished a year of teaching and need a break. I've planned a wonderful holiday traveling in Australia and New Zealand and everything's paid for. And last, and perhaps most important, having once been your girlfriend I've no desire to be—"

Jesslyn wasn't able to finish the rest, drowned out by the blare of the school fire alarm.

It was a loud, piercing sound, and for a moment Jesslyn stood transfixed. Normally she'd snag her attendance book and swiftly march the students out, but there were no young charges to lead to safety.

The door to the classroom flew open and two hulking men appeared, dressed in dark clothes, their weapons cocked and ready. One of them spoke quickly, loudly to Sharif who just nodded and looked back at Jesslyn.

"Happen often?" he shouted over the deafening blare.

"No," she shouted back, reaching for her purse, briefcase and blazer, momentarily taken aback by the quick action of Sharif's security detail, but not totally surprised as Sharif had security even when they lived in London.

"I imagine it's a false alarm," she added distractedly. "One of those end-of-year student pranks the graduating seniors like to pull. But we still have to leave until the fire inspector gives us the okay to return."

She'd just lifted her blazer from the back of her chair when the ceiling sprinklers came on, drenching the classroom in a torrent of warm water.

Sharif grabbed her briefcase and purse from her desk. "Let's go."

The hallway connecting the classrooms was slick with water, and as they dashed down the hall they could hear sirens in the distance and a lot of yelling in Arabic.

By the time they reached the front steps of the main administrative building, the fire trucks were pulling into the parking lot and the rest of Sharif's security team, another half-dozen men, were on full alert.

As his men spotted Sharif they moved toward him, but Sharif quickly checked their progress.

Dr. Maddox, who'd been pacing the school's front steps,

rushed toward them. "I'm sorry," she said, wringing the hem of her skirt and then her hands. "I'm so terribly sorry about all this. We pride ourselves on our school and yet here you are, absolutely soaked—"

"We're all soaked," Sharif said, "and we'll dry." He glanced past her to the school where the firemen had gone to do a formal check to make sure there wasn't a fire anywhere. "Miss Heaton's classroom was drenched. Are all classrooms that wet?"

"I imagine they are. It's a new sprinkler system, put in this year on recommendation by our school board. And they work—" Dr. Maddox paused, pushed back wet gray hair from her forehead "—a little too well."

"But it's worth it if it'll save lives," Jesslyn interjected as she took her things from Sharif. "We can replace books and carpeting, and fortunately the school is insured. With nearly three months before classes resume, there's time to fix everything."

"Are you volunteering to give up your holiday, Miss Heaton?" Dr. Maddox asked irritably. "Because to get everything done, someone will have to be here overseeing the repairs."

"Miss Heaton has plans, I believe," Sharif answered smoothly, and turning his back on Dr. Maddox he focused his full attention on Jesslyn. "I'll walk you to your car."

"I don't have a car," she said, shouldering the strap of her purse. "I take a taxi home."

Sharif frowned. "But you drive."

"Cars are expensive, and I'm happy taking taxis. No one bothers me." And no one would, she knew, not in Sharjah.

Jesslyn loved her adopted country. Sharjah might not have the same glittering nightlife of Dubai or the mad hustle bustle of the business world, but it retained a charm and elegance not found so easily in Dubai's sleek skyscraper-studded skyline and artificial island paradise.

In her mind Sharjah was quieter, smaller, less splash and cash. She adored the stately palm-tree-lined boulevards and the handsome tall buildings in the center. It was always a pleasure to walk or take a taxi to wherever she needed to go. And she didn't have to worry about the parking, either. She felt welcome here. Welcome and wanted.

"I'll take you home, then," Sharif announced, and with a nod toward his guards, he indicated he was ready to leave. "My car is waiting just there."

Jesslyn had already spotted the limousine and two black escort vehicles, but she wasn't about to accept a ride. "I'd prefer to hail a taxi," she answered, with a swift glance at her wristwatch. "And if I leave now, I can just avoid the afternoon rush hour."

She's walking away.

Walking away from me.

Incredulous, King Sharif Fehr bit down so hard he felt as if he was choking on his own tongue, but it was that or say something he might regret.

Not that he thought he'd regret it.

In fact, right now he was certain he'd derive a great deal of pleasure from putting Jesslyn Heaton in her place.

"I shall take you," he repeated, teeth flashing in a barely civil smile. "I insist."

Her brown eyes lifted, met his. He saw her full lips compress, her mouth a dark rose.

Hot sparks lit her eyes. Leaning forward she whispered so only he could hear. "I do not work for you, King Fehr, nor am I one of your subjects. You can't insist. I'm afraid you forget, Your Highness, that you have no jurisdiction over me."

Once again she'd told him no. Once again she'd flat-out rejected him.

He frowned, trying to digest her rejection.

It'd been years since anyone had refused him so absolutely. People didn't say no to him. People needed him. People came to him wanting favors, assistance, support.

Studying her pale, oval-shaped face, he let his gaze drift from her dark, winged eyebrows to the heat in her warm eyes to the set of her firmly molded chin. He'd never noticed just how firm that chin was until now. He'd never noticed her backbone until now, either.

When he'd first known her she'd been a broken girl, literally broken from the accident that had taken his sisters. Jesslyn had been in the hospital, all white plaster and gauze and pins.

She wasn't broken anymore.

"You don't like me," he said, almost amused. On one hand he was angered by her cool dismissal, and on the other hand he was surprised and intrigued, which was a novelty in and of itself. As king of a Middle Eastern country enjoying its tenth year of peace and economic stability, these days he found himself surprised by little and intrigued by even less.

Jesslyn eyed him steadily, her feelings for him definitely mixed. "Perhaps it would be more accurate to say I don't trust you."

"Why on earth wouldn't you trust me?"

She again shouldered her purse, her damp coat dripping over her arm. "You're not the Sharif I knew. You're King Fehr."

"*Jesslyn.*" His voice suddenly dropped, turned coaxing. He didn't like his integrity being questioned. "Obviously, I've offended you. That wasn't my intention. I've come to you to ask for help. At least let me explain."

She glanced toward his limousine and then his half-dozen men who stood at attention, their eyes shielded by dark glasses. "I'm catching a redeye flight tonight, and I'm going to be on that plane."

"So you'll let me drive you home?"

She turned her head, looked up at him, her damp dark hair forming soft ringlets around her face. "I'm going to be on that plane," she repeated.

He liked the way the dark-chestnut curls framed her pale face, liked the stubborn press of her lips and the defiant lift of her chin. "Then let me take you home."

CHAPTER TWO

AFTER giving Sharif's driver her address, Jesslyn placed her purse and briefcase on the floor and laid her damp coat on her damp lap as she tried to ignore the fact that Sharif was sitting so close.

Unfortunately, he was impossible to ignore. He was the kind of man who dominated a room, drawing light, attention, energy. And worse, sitting so close to him she could feel his warmth, smell a hint of his fragrance, and it threw her back to the past, filling her with memories of his skin. She loved his skin. He'd always known how to hold her.

Her heart turned over, and her fingers curled into her coat as the strangest pain shot through her.

Sorrow. Grief. Regret.

He was awakening memories and feelings she didn't want or need, memories and feelings of a past—a life—she'd accepted was gone.

"You don't look at me," he said, as the car started.

She couldn't exactly tell him that looking at him made her hurt worse. Made her realize all over again how foolish she'd been when she'd left him. She hadn't really meant to walk away, not forever. Instead she'd thought he would have come running after her, had hoped he would have pursued her, beg her to reconsider, pledge undying love.

"Endings are awkward. It was awkward then, and it's awkward now."

"But you're happier. Look at you. You're living your dream."

Her dream. She inhaled softly, a quick gasp of protest. She'd never dreamed of being single at her age. Her dream had always been to have a family, a family of her own. Having been raised by an elderly aunt after her parents' deaths—three years apart—made her realize how much she needed people to love and people to love her. Instead here she was still single, and still teaching other peoples' children.

"Yes," she agreed, hiding the pain his words caused her. "It's wonderful."

"I've never seen you this confident," he added.

Jesslyn glanced out the window and watched the fire trucks and school buildings fall away as the limousine exited the parking lot and pulled onto the street. "It's not hard being stronger or more confident," she said after a moment, turning to look at him. "All those years ago I was a different person."

He knew immediately what she alluded to. His eyes darkened. "It was a terrible accident."

She nodded, and suddenly the accident wasn't eleven years ago, but yesterday, and the loss was just as fresh. "I still dream about it sometimes," she said, knotting her hands, her fingers interlocking so tightly the tips of her fingers shone pink and the knuckles white. "I always wake up on impact. I wake up before I know what's happened."

Sharif didn't speak, and she fought the enormous heaviness bearing down on her chest. "But when I wake I know what happened."

"You weren't at the wheel."

"But Jamila did nothing wrong. No one in our car did anything wrong."

"That's why they're called accidents."

Tragedies, she whispered in her mind.

"Otherwise, you've healed," he said. "You're lucky."

His sisters hadn't been.

Hot tears stung her eyes, and Jesslyn swiftly reached up and brushed them away before they could fall. It'd been a long time since she'd talked about the accident, and still she carried the grief and loss in her heart. Jamila and Aman had been her best friends. She'd met them when she was ten, and they'd become instantly inseparable.

But the past was the past, she reminded herself, trying to focus on the present. She could only live right now, in the present time, a time where she could actually make a difference. "You've changed, too, but I suppose you had to, being a…"

"Yes?" he prompted when her voice faded away without finishing the thought.

Jesslyn shifted uncomfortably. "You know."

"But I don't. Why don't you tell me."

She didn't miss the ruthless edge in his voice, and suddenly she wished she'd never said anything at all. "You have to know you've changed," she said, dodging his question even as she looked at him, really looked at him and saw all over again how much harder, fiercer, prouder he'd become. Beautiful silver into steel.

"You don't like me now, though."

Her shoulders shifted. "I don't know you now."

"I'm still the same person."

But he wasn't, she thought, he wasn't the man she knew. He'd become something other, larger, more powerful, and more conscious of that power, too. "Maybe what I should say is that I don't see the man anymore, I see the king." She could see from the hardening of his expression that he didn't like what she'd said, so she hastily added, "But of course you've changed. You're not a young man anymore. You're now... what? Thirty-eight, thirty-nine?"

"Thirty-seven, Miss Heaton." He paused, his voice deepening. "And you're thirty-one."

Something in his voice made her look up, and when she did, she stared straight into his stunning silver-gray eyes, eyes she'd once found heartbreakingly beautiful.

Eyes that seemed to pierce her heart now.

The air left her in a rush, forcing her to take a quick breath and then another.

Her prince had become a king. Her Sharif had married and then been widowed. Her own life with him had been a lifetime ago.

"You're displeased with me, and yet it's the opposite for me. You're more than I remembered," he continued in the same deep, husky voice, "more confident. More beautiful. More of everything."

Once again her chest tightened, her heart feeling as mashed as a potato.

He made her feel too much. He made her remember everything.

Inexplicably she suddenly wanted to seize all the years back, the nine years she'd buried herself in good works and deeds, the years in higher-education courses and summer school and night school, arduous activities and pursuits designed to keep her from thinking or feeling.

Designed to keep her from regretting.

Prince Sharif Fehr, her Prince Sharif Fehr, her first lover, her only love, had married someone else only months after they broke off.

Shifting restlessly, she glanced out the window, saw they were less than a mile from her apartment and felt confusing emotions of disappointment and relief.

Soon he'd drop her off and be gone.

Soon she could be in control of her emotions again.

Sharif's gaze still rested on her face. "So tell me more about your school, your current job. Are you happy there? What is the faculty like?"

This Jesslyn could answer easily, with a clear conscience. "I love being a teacher. I always end up so attached to my students, and I still get a thrill teaching literature and history. And yes, the school is very different from the American School in London, and the American School in Dubai where I taught one year, but I have a lot more control over my curriculum here and I get to spend more time with my students, which is what I want."

"*Your* students," he repeated.

She smiled, finally able to breathe easier. Talking about teaching put her firmly back in control of her emotions, and she wanted to keep it that way. She *had* to keep it that way. "I do think of them as my kids, but I can't help it. I have such high hopes for each of them."

"If you love children so much, why don't you have any of your own?"

Immediately she was thrown back into inner chaos, her sense of calm and goodwill vanishing. *Did his mother never tell him? Did he still really not know?*

Her fingers balled into fists as she felt anger wash through her, anger toward his cold, manipulative mother, and anger toward Sharif. Sharif was supposed to have loved her. Sharif was supposed to have wanted her.

"Haven't met the right person," she answered tightly, looking into his face, seeing again the hard, carved features, the way his dark sleek hair touched his robe, and the shadow of a beard darkening his jaw.

That face…

His eyes…

Heat rushed through her, heat followed by ice because she could never have been his wife. She could never have been the one he married and cherished. She was, as his mother had put it so indelicately, a good-time girl. Someone frivolous and fun to pass the time with.

"You've never married?" he asked.

"No."

"I'm surprised. When you left all those years ago I was sure there was someone, or something, you wanted."

No, there was nothing else she wanted, but she hadn't known how to fight then. Hadn't known how to keep, protect, what she loved. "We're almost to my apartment," she said numbly, gesturing to the street.

"My girls need a teacher this summer. They're home from boarding school and lagging academically."

They were so close to her apartment, so close. Just another block and she could get out, run away, escape.

"I'll pay you three times your annual salary," he continued. "In ten weeks you could make three times what you make in a year."

She wanted to cover her ears. She didn't want to know about the job, didn't want to hear about his children—children he'd had with his fabulously wealthy and stunningly beautiful princess—or their academic deficiencies. "I'm going on holiday, Sharif. I leave tonight."

"I thought you cared about children. I thought you wanted what's best for children."

But these weren't her children and she wasn't going to get involved. "I've plans," she repeated woodenly.

"Plans you could change," Sharif said so pleasantly that Jesslyn felt a prickle beneath her skin. She didn't trust Sharif when he used that tone of voice.

But then, she didn't trust Sharif at all.

Maybe that's because she didn't know the real Sharif. The Sharif she'd dated and adored would have never married a Dubai princess just to further his career and kingdom, much less married that princess less than six months after they'd broken up. But that's what he'd done. His wedding had been covered by virtually every glossy magazine in the UK, and in every article about the wedding, below every photograph the caption read, *Prince Sharif Fehr Marries Princess Zulima of Dubai after a Year-Long Engagement.*

Year-long engagement?

Impossible. Six months before the wedding Jesslyn was still dating Sharif.

The car had stopped but Jesslyn didn't wait for the driver to appear. Gathering her things, she flung the door open. "Good luck, Sharif," she said, sliding her legs out and standing. "Goodbye."

And Jesslyn rushed to the entrance of her building, racing to the lobby and the entrance as though her life depended on it. And in a way it did, because Sharif would annihilate her if she gave him the chance.

She wouldn't give him the chance.

In her apartment Jesslyn forced herself to focus on finishing packing. She wasn't going to think about Sharif, not again, not anymore. She had more pressing things to think about, things like her passport, sunscreen and extra batteries for her digital camera.

Her trip required more luggage than she would normally take, but ten weeks and radically different climates meant swimsuits and shorts for the warmer temperatures in Northern Queensland, slacks and elegant blouses for the big Australian cities, and then down jackets and fleece-lined boots for the ski slopes in New Zealand.

She was just zipping the biggest suitcase closed when her phone rang.

"Hello," Jesslyn said, answering the phone as she dragged her big suitcase into the hall.

It was Sharif. "I've news I thought you'd want to hear."

She straightened, leaving the suitcase by her door. "I've a million things to do before the flight, Sharif—"

"It concerns one of your students." He hesitated. "Perhaps you'd like to sit down."

"Why?" she asked suspiciously. "What's happened?"

"I just had a call from Mahir, my chief of security, and he's on his way to the Sharjah police station. They've arrested one of the school students for vandalizing the campus this afternoon. It was thought that I'd want to press charges."

She walked into the small living room and leaned against the back of her couch. "Are you pressing charges?"

"Mahir is handling the matter."

"But what does that mean?"

"It means that Mahir makes those decisions. He's responsible for my security."

Jesslyn's hand shook as she held the phone to her ear. "Which student?"

"Aaron."

Aaron?

She frowned, bewildered. It couldn't have been Aaron. Aaron wasn't like that. Aaron didn't pull pranks. He was a good kid, a serious kid, almost nerdy. "He didn't do it," she said faintly, folding one arm across her chest to fight the icy weakness in her limbs. "He wouldn't pull the fire alarm. He wouldn't."

"They caught him running from the scene."

"It just…it's not…it's not what he'd do…" And then her voice faded as she pictured the small gift Aaron had brought her earlier that day, after school had ended. She could see the white paper, the colorful silk ribbon. She'd left it on her desk when the sprinklers turned on.

"Wait." Jesslyn chewed on her mouth. "He *was* on campus after school, but that's because he had a goodbye gift for me. He's moving back to the States."

"Which probably explains his stunt," Sharif answered. "I may be in my thirties but I remember being a teenager, and kids do things to get attention—"

"So you will forgive him?" she interrupted eagerly.

"If that's all he did, the punishment would be light. But he didn't just pull the fire alarm. Apparently he also broke into the vice principal's office and stole copies of exams from a filing cabinet. Dr. Maddox intends to prosecute." He paused. "She's asked me to press charges as well."

"Don't," she whispered.

"It's not just me, though. The police are involved, as well. Theft is a serious crime."

Swallowing, Jesslyn felt her heart lodge up in her throat. There was absolutely no way Aaron did what they said he'd done. "Sharif, he didn't steal anything. He brought me a gift. It's on my desk. We can go to school, retrieve that—"

"A janitor spotted the boy running away."

"He was running to get home, not running away!"

"Jesslyn, there's nothing we can do right now."

She continued to shake her head. It wasn't true. She wouldn't believe it until she talked to Aaron herself. "I must see him. Take me to the jail, Sharif, please take me right now."

"They won't allow you to see him. They've called his parents, but the police must finish questioning him first."

Jesslyn closed her eyes and drew a deep breath. "You're telling me they won't let you in? You're telling me they won't let Sheikh Sharif Fehr in to see a child?"

He sighed. *"Jesslyn."*

Her heart was racing so hard it hurt. "You can get me in to see him, Sharif."

Silence stretched over the phone line. "I know how protective you are of your students—"

"Sharif. Please." Her voice broke. "Please."

Again silence answered her request, a silence that just grew longer, heavier until she heard him sigh again. "I'll send my car for you, *laeela*, but understand this is serious. Understand he's being formally charged."

Sharif's car arrived for her within the hour, and while sitting in the back of the dark Mercedes sedan, Jesslyn replayed the afternoon scene with Aaron in her mind again and again.

He'd been upset when he gave her the gift, touchingly emotional. But had he been acting? Or was it a ruse? The gift of the present an opportunity to cover his crime?

She didn't know and still couldn't decide when the car pulled up in front of the station. Sharif was already there, appearing from the police station to meet her at the car.

Jesslyn had changed before the car arrived for her, selecting a conservative, loose-fitting chocolate linen dress with long sleeves and a simple skirt. It was a dress she wore when she didn't want to draw attention to her figure as she knew both men and women traditionally wore robes to hide the body. Sharif, she noticed, had changed, too.

He offered his hand to her as she stepped from the car. She didn't want to take it but couldn't refuse him, not with so many of his men watching.

Reluctantly she put her hand in his, felt his fingers wrap around hers.

"You're cold," Sharif said, as she stepped onto the pavement.

"I'm nervous," she confessed, worriedly glancing up into the sky. It was beginning to grow dark. Her flight would board in a little more than three hours.

His expression sharpened. "You think he did do it, then?"

"No." She shot Sharif a desperate look. "I'm certain he didn't, but I'm afraid for him. If his parents have been called they'll be upset. He'll be upset." She shook her head. "Oh, I wish none of this had happened."

"But it has. Now we just have to see what the situation is."

They headed for the police station's entrance, Sharif's security detail surrounding them. The bodyguards were everywhere tonight—in front of them, behind them, beside them, and while the security had been with them earlier today, it unnerved her tonight.

Or maybe it was Sharif who was unnerving her by walking so close.

Inside the station Sharif was received with great respect. The entire station staff, from desk sergeants to detectives to the chief of police, made a point of welcoming Sharif, and after ten minutes of warm greetings, the police chief and Sharif stepped aside to have a private talk.

Jesslyn waited anxiously for them to return, praying that Sharif could convince the police chief to let her see Aaron. Finally Sharif summoned her. "We have been granted permission to speak to your student, and you may ask him whatever you'd like, but you must understand they've a good case against him." He looked at her, his gray gaze shuttered. "Jesslyn, the consequences would be severe."

Another one of her fears.

Sharjah was Jesslyn's second home and she was loath to criticize any of it, much less the government and the very good police force that worked so hard to protect both Western expats and Arab citizens, but there were dangers here, particularly for careless or reckless American teenagers who failed to heed the law.

Fortunately, teenage boys didn't go to prison for stealing or destroying private property, but the punishment wouldn't be light and could be emotionally scarring.

"I understand," she whispered.

They were escorted to a small office, and while they waited for Aaron, Jesslyn nervously twisted the ring on her third finger, a ring given to her by her grandmother when she'd turned eighteen. She'd always called it her good luck ring and she played with it now, praying for good fortune.

The door finally opened and the police chief appeared, escorting young Aaron.

She was devastated that he was handcuffed, but before she could say a word the police chief removed the boy's handcuffs and pulled out a chair for him.

Aaron tumbled into the chair, his head hung so low he couldn't see anything but the floor.

"Aaron." She said his name softly.

His head lifted slightly but she could at least see his face.

He'd been crying. His cheeks still bore traces of tears and his nose was red and shiny. "Miss Heaton," he choked.

Her heart contracted. He'd always been one of her favorite students and to see him like this made her feel absolutely desperate. She didn't even know what to say.

As if he could read her mind he shook his head. "I didn't do it, Miss Heaton. I swear I didn't. It wasn't me. It wasn't."

She wanted to comfort him but didn't know how, not when she knew she couldn't reassure him that everything would be fine. It was impossible to promise him anything. "They found you on campus," she said carefully. "They said they caught you running."

He groaned. "I was on campus because I'd taken you a gift."

"But why were you running?"

"I was late getting home. I didn't want my father to know I'd missed the school bus."

She bit her bottom lip, bit down to keep her emotions in check. "Apparently someone saw you running from the office—"

"Not me." He looked at her, eyes brilliant with unshed tears. "And maybe someone was running from the office, and maybe someone had stolen papers, but it wasn't me."

Sharif glanced from Jesslyn to the boy. "What do you know about the papers?"

Aaron's jaw hardened and yet his eyes were filled with pain. "I can't tell you."

"Why not?"

"I can't." And then he dropped his head, his shoulders slumping.

Jesslyn moved forward on her chair. "Aaron, if you know who did it, it would save you from serious trouble."

"And if I tell you, he'd be in serious trouble and I can't do that. His mom is already dying—" Aaron broke off on a soft sob. His head hung so low that a tear fell and dropped onto the floor.

Jesslyn inhaled sharply, knowing who he was referring to. Only one boy in the upper grades had a mom dying, and it was Will. Will McInnes. Will's mother had just been moved to a hospice facility, and Will's father was coping by drinking too much and then terrorizing the children.

She turned to Sharif. "I need to talk to you." They stepped out of the room and stood in the narrow hall.

She told Sharif everything, about Will and Aaron's friendship, how Aaron's parents had done their best to include Will in their family life as Will's family life unraveled. "Will is barely getting by," she said, her eyes stinging. "He's had such a hard year, and the only person who's really been there for him is Aaron. And now Aaron's leaving."

"But why steal?" Sharif replied. "And why pull the alarm? He flooded the school, which destroyed nearly every classroom. He's going to have a criminal record and his family will have to pay for the damage, damage that will be in the thousands."

"Then we can't tell anyone it was Will. We'll deal with Will ourselves."

"*We* will?" Sharif repeated.

"We *have* to. His dad has a fierce temper. I can't bear to think what he'd do to Will if he found out about this afternoon."

"So you'll let Aaron, who just might be innocent, pay for the crime instead?"

Jesslyn could picture Aaron in her mind, could see his ashen face and the tear that trembled on his lower lash before spilling and falling to the cement in a wet plop. "No. We get Aaron off."

"Jesslyn."

She lifted her shoulders. "He didn't do it, he can't be punished. Will did do it—"

"So he should be punished."

"But he's a child, Sharif, in the process of losing his mother. She doesn't have long. Not even a month. It's all about pain management for her now, and imagine what Will is going through, imagine how helpless he feels, imagine his rage."

Sharif gazed down into Jesslyn's upturned face.

It wasn't hard for him to imagine what Will was going through, he thought, nor was it difficult to imagine the grief, the fury, the pain as his children had lost their mother just three years ago. Unlike Will's mother, Zulima's death had been sudden, and there had been no time for goodbyes. One moment she was resting in her room after her cesarian section and the next gone, dying from a blood clot.

"My children also lost their mother," he said roughly. "It's not fair for children to lose their mother so early in life, but it does happen."

"But if we can do something, change something, make it more fair—"

"We can't."

"We can." She took his arm with both her hands, pleading. "Please, Sharif. Please help me help these children. Get Aaron released. Help me find Will, let me speak with him. Perhaps we can get the papers back, get them returned."

"You're asking for a miracle."

Her hands gripped his arm tighter. "Then give me a miracle, Sharif. If anyone can make this happen, you can. You can do anything. You always could."

Sharif stared down into her upturned face, fascinated by the pink bloom in her cheeks and dusky rose of her lips. Emotion lit her features; passion and conviction darkened her eyes.

She looked at him with such faith. She looked at him with

all the confidence in the world. She was so certain he could do all this, certain he *would*.

Her fierce faith in him made his breath catch. Her fire made something in his chest hurt. In all his years of marriage Zulima had never once looked at him that way.

"I'd have to pull a million strings," he said, even as his brain already worked through the possibilities of getting Aaron released and Will sorted out. It'd be complicated, far from easy, but he did know the right people and he could put in calls…

"Then pull them," she answered, dark-brown brows knitting.

"It's more than a snap of my fingers," he answered, intrigued by this Jesslyn Heaton standing in front of him. This woman was neither naive nor helpless. In fact, this Jesslyn Heaton had grown into something of a warrior and a defender of the young.

"I understand that, but I love these kids and I know these kids. I've taught them for years. Will's acting out and Aaron's protecting him, and yet in the end, they're just boys. Just children."

He'd never heard any other woman but Jesslyn speak with so much feeling, but that was the kind of woman Jesslyn had always been. From the time he met her she wore her heart on her sleeve, and eleven years after first meeting her he realized her heart was still there for everyone to see.

Impulsively he reached out and touched her smooth, flushed cheek. Her skin was warm and surprisingly soft. He dropped his hand quickly and hardened himself to her pleas. "It'd be better to let the boys take the blame and accept the consequences. That way they'd learn from this."

"Maybe," she argued, "maybe in other circumstances they would learn. But not now, not when Will's mom is nearly gone." She held his gaze, held it long, her expression beseeching. "Do this for me, Sharif, do this and I will do whatever I can for you."

His pulse quickened. His interest sharpened. "What exactly are you offering?"

Shadows chased through her eyes, shadows of worry and mistrust, and then she shook her head and her expression cleared. "You need me," she said firmly. "You came to me today because you wanted me for the summer. Well…" her voice wavered for a moment before she pressed on. "Help me sort the boys out, and then I will help you for the next two weeks—"

"No. Not two weeks. The summer."

The clouds were back in her eyes, and some of the pink faded from her cheeks. "But the trip. My trip…"

"So what do you want more? Your holiday or your children rescued?"

She stared up at him, her lips pressing grimly, and he could see her thoughts, could see her frustration and resentment but also the realization that he alone could do what she needed, wanted, done.

"You love children," he added quietly, surprised by the sudden tightness in his chest. Pressure and pain. "And my children need you. My children need you as much as these two."

And still she looked up at him, weighing, judging, deciding. She didn't trust him, he could see it in her eyes and that alone made him want to drag her back to Sarq. She was the one who had betrayed him, not the other way around. She had no right to mistrust him. He was the one who'd been deceived.

He was the one who was owed not just an apology but the truth. And he'd have the truth. After nine years he was going to have that truth.

Jesslyn touched the tip of her tongue to her upper lip. "So, if I give you the summer, you will make this problem go away?"

"The entire summer," he said.

If Jesslyn felt any trepidation she didn't show it. Instead her eyes flashed and her chin jutted up. "We have a deal, then?"

His lashes dropped and his gaze drifted slowly across her face. "Your head for his?" He paused, considered her. "I don't know if it's fair, but I'll take it."

CHAPTER THREE

AN HOUR and a half later Sharif stood in the shadows of the McInnes house and listened to Jesslyn give Will McInnes the talking to of a lifetime.

If Sharif hadn't heard Jesslyn's severe tone, he wouldn't have known she had it in her. But apparently she did, for she let Will know in no uncertain terms that she knew what he had done, and he was in serious trouble.

Not only did she want all the stolen tests back—tonight— but he should also consider himself on probation. If he so much as broke a pencil or stepped on a bug, she'd have his head. That is, if she didn't go to his father right now and tell him what Will had done this afternoon.

When Jesslyn returned to the car twenty minutes later, she carried a stack of exams and handed them to Sharif before getting in the car. "There. Yours. Mission completed."

"You weren't easy on him," he said.

Seated in the car Jesslyn sighed and rubbed the back of her neck, her head aching. The day felt positively endless. "No, I wasn't. I was angry and disappointed, and I let him know it."

One of the guards closed the door behind her. "Is that why he was crying when he brought you the tests?" Sharif asked.

Her lips pursed. "He was crying because I told him if he ever did anything stupid like that again that you'd have him arrested and thrown into prison, and who knew what would happen to his family."

Sharif's eyebrows lifted. "You didn't."

"I did." She wrinkled her nose as she reflected on what she'd said and done. "Was that so terrible?"

"Not if you can save him from a life of crime."

"My thoughts exactly." She turned to look out the tinted window. The limousine was again winding through the quiet downtown streets, but this time they were heading the opposite direction from which they'd come, away from her apartment and on toward Dubai. "We're not going back to my apartment?"

"No. We're going to stay at a hotel in Dubai tonight and then fly out in the morning."

"But my things…"

"I've taken care of that. A courier picked your suitcase and travel bag up from your apartment. You'd left both by the front door."

She shot him a cool glance. "You left nothing to chance."

The corner of his mouth lifted, but it wasn't much of a smile. "I try not to."

So that was that, she thought. There'd be no holiday this summer. Instead she was going back to work.

Tired tears started to come, but she squeezed her eyes closed, forced them away, refusing to feel sorry for herself. She'd done the right thing. She knew she had. How could she possibly have gone on holiday when Aaron would have faced horrible fines and stiff charges? Better to miss some beaches and skiing and live with a clear conscience.

"You must be hungry," Sharif said, his voice deep in the

car's dark interior. "It's nearing eleven, and I can't imagine you've eaten since noon."

"No, but I haven't been hungry. Too many emotions," she answered, sinking back deeper against the impossibly soft leather seat. She was tired and thirsty and virtually numb from the roller-coaster day.

When she'd woken up this morning she'd thought she would be flying to Brisbane tonight. Instead the plane had taken off without her and she was facing the prospect of a long summer in Sarq.

The thought alone sent prickles of fresh panic up and down her spine.

How could she do this? How could she spend ten weeks with Sharif and his family? The fact that he was widowed changed nothing for her.

"I know nothing about this job I've accepted," she said. "You'll have to tell me about your children. How many...their names, their ages, as well as your objectives."

"I will," he answered. "But first things first, and that's a proper dinner, because I know you—you need to eat. You always skimp meals to get things done, but in the end, it backfires. You just end up irritable."

"I don't."

"You do. And you are already. You should see your face. You're famished and exhausted."

She bit back her immediate retort. It wouldn't help to get into a hissing contest with Sharif. The fact was, they were going to spend a considerable amount of time together. Better to try to get along with him than become adversaries. "So, distract me from my hunger. Tell me something about your family. How many children will I be teaching?"

"Three."

"Boys and girls, all boys…?"

"All girls." His expression never outwardly changed, but Jesslyn sensed tension and didn't know why or what it was.

"They're bilingual?" she asked, knowing her Arabic would get her by on market day but wouldn't be considered proper Arabic by any stretch of the imagination.

"Yes, but you'll discover all that tomorrow when we head home."

Home. His home. Sarq. A country she'd visited only once, and very briefly, to attend Aman's funeral. She'd flown in and out the same day, and in her grief, she remembered nothing but the heat. It was summer after all and hot, so very very hot.

But they weren't in Sarq yet. No, they were heading for the glossy and busy city-state of Dubai.

A 200-year-old city, once populated by pirates and smugglers, today Dubai was a cosmopolitan melting pot, teeming with more foreigners than locals. The city had blossomed overnight with the discovery of oil and now had so much money that the powers that be kept coming up with the most interesting ways to put it all back into the country and boost tourism. Jesslyn hadn't quite gotten used to the idea of man-made islands shaped like the world, or the snow ski facility in the desert. There were already plans underway for a huge theme park called Dubailand, along the lines of Disneyland and even an underwater hotel.

Dubai Creek ran through the middle of the city-state with the business district Deira to the east, and Bur Dubai, the commercial and historic district, to the west.

But the driver wasn't going to Deira or Bur Dubai, he was destined for Jumeriah Beach, the playland for the rich, royal and beautiful.

Despite living in the Emirates for six years Jesslyn had

spent very little time at Jumeriah Beach's posh waterfront resorts. For one, you couldn't even get into some of the hotels unless you were a hotel guest, and "treating" oneself to a night at the Burj Al Arab, reportedly the most luxurious hotel in the world, wasn't in the budget, not when rooms started at $1,280. But obviously that wasn't a problem for a man with Sharif's wealth.

"We're eating here?" she asked Sharif as the car turned into the hotel's private drive.

"And staying here. I've my own suite reserved for my exclusive use."

"That's nice."

He merely smiled at her, the smile of a king who'd become used to having his way.

As they stepped from the car, Jesslyn felt as if she'd entered a production of *Arabian Nights*: gilded doors magically opened, overhead lights dimmed, lush green fronds parted.

The uniformed staff scrambled to assist Sharif, and while Jesslyn knew hotel staff were exceptionally attentive in Dubai, she personally found the attention overwhelming. There were too many people, too much bowing, too much of everything.

"You'll have your own suite," Sharif said. "And the hotel manager has promised to see you there and make sure you've everything you need."

Jesslyn glanced around. "My luggage—"

The hotel manager nodded. "It's already there, ma'am."

While Sharif took one elevator, she took another, escorted by the hotel manager and a young woman in a fashionable robe and veil. The hotel manager described the hotel, explained where everything was, including the numerous restaurants and lounges. "You'll have your own butler," he added, gesturing to the veiled young woman, "and anything you should need will be taken care of. Also, you will be dining with His Highness in thirty minutes. Meena will escort you to the restaurant where you'll be joining Sheikh Fehr."

Jesslyn barely had time for a quick bath, a change into a simple black skirt topped by a soft silk pearl-gray blouse and a quick brush of her hair before it was time to go.

She followed the robed woman back to the elevator where they went to a lower level, transferred to a different elevator, which went straight to the restaurant at the very top of the luxurious hotel.

Jesslyn had to skirt a group of robed men who were in animated discussion. She caught bits and pieces of the conversation—impossible not to as they were talking quite loudly—and discovered their conversation had to do with Sheikh Fehr. Apparently two or more of the men had daughters and each father was quite adamant that it was his daughter who would be marrying King Fehr next September.

Jesslyn froze and stiffened as though she'd just been doused with a bucket of ice water.

Was Sharif getting married again? Were plans in the works for another Dubai princess?

Her head practically throbbed. Jesslyn put a hand to her temple, closed her eyes, wondering all over again just what kind of personal hell she'd agreed to. Tragically, she had no one else to blame for her situation. She'd agreed to this scenario. Had offered herself up.

Her ridiculous morals and values. Her ridiculous Joan of Arc complex!

One day she'd wise up. One day she'd put herself first, protect herself first.

"Headache?" a deep voice murmured at her elbow. Lifting her head, Jesslyn looked up into Sharif's face.

The lashes fringing his silver eyes were thick and black. Strong cheekbones jutted above an equally strong jaw.

"Terrible," she admitted, but unwilling to tell him that he was the source of her tension.

"Food will help and they have our table waiting."

Sharif signaled to the maître d' that they were ready, and immediately the host showed them to a prime window table with a view of the entire city where skyscrapers glittered in every direction.

Sharif ordered several appetizers to be brought right away as well as platters for dinner. "Eat," Sharif said when the first of the appetizers arrived, pushing the small plates of seasoned meat, fish and assorted flat breads toward her. "You'll feel better."

But eating in front of Sharif was almost impossible. Even though the dishes were superbly prepared, chewing and swallowing required a Herculean effort, and after a few more bites of food Jesslyn gave up.

Sharif had watched her attempt to eat and now observed her pushing her food around her plate. "Have you developed one of those eating disorders? You never had a problem with food before."

Jesslyn was grateful to drop the pretense. "It's been a long day and a hard day. I thought I'd be on a plane right now and instead…" Her voice drifted off and, looking across the table at Sharif, she gave her head a slight, bemused shake. "It's hard to take in, hard to accept."

Just saying the words filled her with fury and resentment. Sharif could have helped her without insisting she give up her holiday. He could have helped her just because he was in a position to be able to help.

"You're upset because I won," he said, his tone deceptively mild.

She turned her head, gave him a long, level look. "Is that what this is to you? A competition? Or better yet, a battle where one person must win and the other loses?"

The edge of his generous mouth curved, and yet his gaze was hard, hot, sharp, and he looked at her so intensely that she felt bolts of electricity shoot through her.

"You haven't yet learned that everything in life is a competition?" he drawled, his deep voice pitched low, his tone lazy, almost indulgent. "Life is just one endless battle after another. It's all about power. It's nothing but a quest for control."

The chemistry between them had always been strong, and even though nearly a decade had passed since she'd last seen him, Jesslyn felt wildly, painfully aware of Sharif.

"Is that what being a king has taught you?"

He suddenly leaned forward, close enough that she could see the sparks of fire and ice in his eyes. "It's what being a man has taught me."

She didn't know if it was his tone or his words but she shifted nervously, strangely self-conscious. Sharif had never made her feel this way before. Anxious. Unsettled. Undone. But then, he'd never been an adversary before and yet somehow it's what he'd become.

Winners and losers, she silently repeated as she crossed her legs beneath the table and accidentally touched his knee with her own. Abruptly she drew back, but not before heat washed through her, heat and embarrassment and a painful awareness.

Their table was too small.

The dining room was too dark.

The atmosphere too charged.

Fortunately just then more food arrived, plates and platters and bowls. Jesslyn thought the food would be a distraction and Sharif would now eat and she'd have a moment to gather her composure. But Sharif threw her all over again with his command.

"You'll serve," he said with such authority that she immediately gritted her teeth.

"Has something happened to your hands?" she flashed, unable to control her burst of temper and defiance.

"You know it's the custom for the woman to serve the man."

"If she has a relationship with or to him. But I am not yours. I don't belong to you—"

"But you do work for me," he interjected softly. "And as one that is now in my employ, it would be proper for you to serve me."

Her chin jerked up and she stared at him in mute fury. He was enjoying this, she thought. He enjoyed having power over her. "Why exactly did you come looking for me today?"

"I needed your help."

But it wasn't just that. It was more than that. She knew it was more because this wasn't the Sharif she'd known. This wasn't a man she'd want to know. "For what?"

He sighed. "You already know this. My children need a tutor. I want you to be their tutor—"

"Then don't treat me like a second-class citizen," she interrupted. "I agreed to teach your children this summer but that doesn't make me your servant or part of the royal staff, and it doesn't mean I'll wait on you or any other member of the royal family."

He held her gaze, his own silver eyes glittering with heat and an emotion she couldn't discern. "Did I upset you by not saying please?"

It was all she could do not to dump her glass of water over his arrogant head as she bit back one angry retort after another. Battling to control her temper, she looked away, out the window to the sparkling lights of the city as it curved to meet the dark sea. A helicopter buzzed past the window on its way to the hotel's landing pad.

"You upset me," she said at length, "by asking me to do something you would have never asked me to do ten years ago." She drew an unsteady breath. "Ten years ago you would have served me."

"We were in London then," he answered.

Her lips lifted in a hard bitter smile. "And you weren't the sheikh." Her head turned and she met his gaze once more. "Isn't that right? This is back to your new philosophy on winning and losing and everything in life being a battle for control."

Sharif reached for the tongs on one of the platters and served himself a generous portion of the lamb and then a scoop of the seafood-laced rice. "There," he said, pushing the bowl of rice toward her. "Consider that a victory. You've won that round."

Jesslyn blinked, her chest hot with bitter emotion. Where had the old Sharif gone, the one who'd once been so kind, so relaxed, so thoughtful?

Shifting in her seat, she accidentally bumped into his leg again beneath the table, his body big, hard, warm, and she nearly ran. She couldn't do this. Couldn't sit here and play nice, not when she remembered how it'd been between them, how he'd once been with her.

She realized that for her the attraction hadn't gone. The old desire hadn't died, and Sharif of ten years ago flashed through her mind—long hair, faded tattered jeans, beach flip-flops on his feet.

As if he knew what she was thinking he said, "I'm not a heartless ogre. I'm not cruel. I care very much about duty, family, responsibility."

Words he would never have used ten years before, at least not like that. From the first time she'd met him, he'd been concerned about his family, concerned about peoples' feelings. He would never have run roughshod over anyone.

Painful memories returned, memories of them as they'd once been—arm in arm walking through Hyde Park, laughing, talking, oblivious to the prince's security detail tailing them everywhere.

Back then Sharif had lived as though he wasn't royal, as though he had only himself to answer to.

He was wrong. And they both knew that. But they could pretend, and they did. For the two and a half years they were together, they pretended....

With an effort she swallowed around the funny lump in her throat. "Now tell me about your girls, their school, everything. Why are you so concerned about them? What is it you want me to do?"

He made a rough sound. "Give me a miracle."

She frowned, not understanding. "What does that mean?"

Sharif didn't immediately answer. Instead he toyed with his spoon, his gaze fixed on a distant point across the restaurant. "I don't actually know what the problem is," he said after a moment. "The girls apparently had considerable problems this year at school, problems I wasn't aware of until they returned home for the summer. The headmistress sent word that it had been a difficult year and she wasn't sure she could have them back, at least, not all of them."

He set the spoon down, pushed it away, his eyes shadowed. "I don't want the girls split up. They've already lost their mother. They shouldn't lose each other."

Jesslyn nodded slightly. She totally agreed with him on that. "Did the headmistress give any specifics about the 'dif-

ficult' year? Were the girls struggling academically or was it
something else?"

"I've looked at their end-of-year marks and they are down
across the board, but it's their conduct marks that trouble me.
My daughters aren't spoiled princesses. They're good girls.
Polite children. And yet it seems the school…the teachers…
have come to view them as troubled."

"Troubled?"

He took a quick rough breath, as though the entire subject
was so painful he could barely endure it. "The youngest had
the worst marks. She essentially failed everything. She's the
one the school isn't sure should return."

Jesslyn waved off the waiter who was trying to refill her
water. "Perhaps it isn't the right school for the girls."

"They've been there for nearly two years."

"Not every school is right for every child."

"My wife attended the same school. It was her desire
they go there."

"How old are your children?"

"Takia is five, Saba is six and Jinan, the eldest, is seven,"
Sharif answered.

"They're babies!"

"My wife went away to boarding school early, too."

Jesslyn had also gone to boarding school in England, but
she'd never enjoyed it, never felt happy about the long school
term and the all-too-brief summer and winter holidays. She'd
also been terribly homesick at first, but she'd adapted. But
then again, she'd been quite a bit older, almost nine when
she'd first gone away. And she hadn't been grieving the loss
of a mother, either.

"Maybe they're too young," she said carefully. "Or maybe
it's too much, too soon after the loss of their mother."

Sharif nodded, jaw flexing. "If that were the case they would be happy now that they're home. But they're not. They're still quite withdrawn. It's as if they've become someone else's children."

"Maybe it's not an academic issue at all."

"I wondered the same thing myself, so I invited a doctor, a specialist in children's mental health issues, to come meet them, spend the day with them, and the doctor said that children go through different adjustment periods and that eventually they'll be fine."

Jesslyn heard the tension and frustration in Sharif's voice. He genuinely cared about his girls. He wanted to help them. He just didn't know how.

He said as much when he continued speaking. "That's why I've come to you. You were always so good with children, even back when you'd just started your teacher training in London. I thought that if anyone could help them, it'd be you."

"Sharif, you know I'm not a therapist, I'm a teacher."

"Yes, and I need you to teach them. Takia can't return with her sisters if she doesn't make up missed and failed coursework, and the other two are struggling in several subjects. You're to teach all of them. They will attend lessons with you every day. I've converted the palace library into a classroom and purchased all the necessary textbooks."

"I haven't taught children as young as yours in years," she reminded him. "My specialty is older children, middle schoolers and high school students, and the curriculum is American based, not UK—"

"That's fine. I've bought teacher's editions, and should you find you require something else, materials, computers, an assistant to help you, just let me know and it's yours."

Why did his reassurance not make her feel better? Why did

that niggle of doubt within her just grow? Was it because elementary education wasn't her area, or because she was afraid of failing when it came to teaching Sharif's children?

"Sharif, I just want to make sure you understand that in this instance, I am not the best teacher for the job. I spend my days teaching literature, grammar, social studies to eleven-through-fourteen-year-olds. I don't teach how to read but how to interpret literary themes, how to deconstruct plot structure, character and conflict." Swallowing quickly she looked up into his eyes. "There are a thousand teachers in Europe more qualified than me—"

"But none more suitable," he answered, leaning forward to touch the back of her hand.

It was a light touch and yet the brush of his fingers across her skin made her breath catch and her belly knot. His touch was still familiar, achingly familiar. For years he had no place in her heart, her mind or her life, and yet in less than twelve hours he'd changed all that.

"What makes me so suitable?" she asked, her voice suddenly husky, colored with emotions and desire she hadn't even known she still could feel. Immediately she fought back, reminding herself, he isn't yours anymore. And you're not his.

But that didn't seem to matter right now, not when she was awash in emotions, stirred by desire. It'd been so easy to be his. It'd felt absolutely natural. And she hadn't known then that what they had was rare and magical. She hadn't known she would never feel that way about anyone again.

Sharif stared across the room, off into the distance, his eyes so striking, his silver-gray irises framed by the densest black lashes with black winged eyebrows beneath a strong forehead. He was her Valentino of the desert.

"There are advantages to being king," he said at last,

speaking slowly, thoughtfully. "It didn't take me long to appreciate those advantages—everyone bows to you, acquiescing to keep you happy. I'm surrounded by people desperate to please me."

He paused, frowned, before continuing. "It's taken me longer to understand the disadvantages. No one wants to earn my disapproval. No one wants to lose a job, a connection, a reward. So people are afraid to tell me unpleasant things and bad news, even if it happens to be the truth."

He turned now to look at her. "Maybe once I wanted that blind obedience, the adoration of my people, but it was a mistake. What I really needed were people who'd give me the truth." His expression shifted, growing troubled and remote. "*Truth*. Whatever it is."

Truth, she repeated silently, mesmerized by the shadows in his gaze. Those shadows hadn't been there when she knew him. When they'd been together, he'd been so bold, so confident, so…free.

But that wasn't the Sharif sitting before her now. No, this man had the weight of the world on his shoulders, weight and worry and a hundred different concerns.

"It hasn't been easy, I take it," she said, remembering how she and Sharif had once loved their evenings and weekends, time for just the two of them, time for long walks and talks followed by a stop at the corner video store and then Chinese or curry take-out. They used to hole up in her apartment and sit on her bed and eat Kung Pao chicken with chopsticks and kiss and laugh.

And laugh.

Looking at Sharif she wondered when he'd last laughed. For that matter, when had she?

But maybe that was all part of growing up. Maybe one

became a full-fledged adult and let all those romantic dreams go....

"I'm not complaining," he answered. "I love my country. I love my children. But nothing is easy, no. There are always compromises. Sacrifices. But you've had those, too, I'm sure." His head turned and he looked at her. "Haven't you?"

CHAPTER FOUR

Despite her sumptuous room with the most amazing Egyptian-cotton linens on the bed, Jesslyn couldn't sleep.

Every time she closed her eyes, she could feel that fleeting brush of Sharif's fingers against the back of her hand, a touch that had scorched her then, a touch that burned her still. But it wasn't just his touch that stayed with her, it was his low voice, a voice that hummed inside her head.

In the dark of her room she felt caught in a time warp, suspended in a moment where they were still together and still very much in love.

After such a fitful night's sleep, the alarm came too early, jarring Jesslyn awake. For a long moment she sat on the edge of her bed, struggling to get her bearings, and then she remembered she was in a hotel room in Dubai waiting for her morning flight to Sarq.

She was going to Sarq to take care of Sharif's children.

Jesslyn very nearly crawled back under the covers to hide but knew it wasn't really an option. Instead she dragged herself into the shower where she turned the faucets on full force.

Drying her hair, she styled it into loose waves to take advantage of her hair's natural curl. Hair done, Jesslyn chose a simple amethyst sheath dress to wear for the flight. The dress had a matching travel coat which she'd carry over her arm.

She was slipping her feet into bone-colored heels when two of Sharif's men arrived at her hotel door. They'd come to take her luggage and escort her to the car. Sharif however wasn't in the car.

"His Highness had an unexpected meeting come up this morning. He'll meet you at the terminal in time for your flight," one of the men said, holding the door for her while the other tucked her luggage into the trunk.

Jesslyn wasn't surprised that Sharif had a meeting come up, and she wasn't surprised that she was traveling to the airport alone, as he was an exceptionally powerful man, but that didn't stop her intense whoosh of disappointment.

The fact that she even felt a whoosh of disappointment scared her. The whoosh meant she still had strong feelings for him. The whoosh meant she cared about his opinion, which made her fear her motivations for taking this job.

The truth was she couldn't afford to get involved with Sharif, not when there was so much history between them.

The truth was she'd gotten involved. There was no backing out of the deal now, not after Sharif had done his part sorting out Aaron's and Will's problems.

The closer the car got to the airport, the more her stomach did crazy flips. Nervously she ran her hands along the slim-fitting skirt of her dress. She'd dressed with such care this morning, had even put on her favorite dress. And yet, wanting to be attractive, wanting him to find her attractive was just asking for trouble.

It was like cutting open an old wound.

She wasn't his girlfriend. She wasn't his equal. She wasn't his colleague. She was just a teacher. The schoolteacher Sharif had hired to mind his royal children for the summer.

The limousine turned through the airport gates, and her stomach did another nosedive. She was here. Her bags were here. Soon she'd be on her way to Sarq, a place she'd wanted to visit for as long as she could remember, and now she was on her way. As Sharif's employee.

Jesslyn swallowed the bitter taste in her mouth as she stepped out of the Mercedes. Sharif's security detail was already there. They ushered her into the beautiful marble-and-glass executive terminal. The very rich and famous used the private terminal, and various sheikhs and businessmen mingled in groups, even as private jets carrying celebrities landed one after the other.

It was a busy terminal, and Jesslyn stood aside just people watching, fascinated by the parade of wealth, glamour and beauty. She was still taking it all in when the exterior doors opened again and another group entered, this group predominantly male with one tall, robed man commanding the most attention.

The atmosphere in the terminal almost instantly changed, charged with a tangible energy, an electric awareness. Heads through the terminal turned, and even Jesslyn felt the frisson of excitement.

Sharif.

She pursed her lips, checking her smile. Wouldn't you know that Sharif could bring a bustling terminal like the Dubai Executive Airport to a standstill.

Even before he was King Fehr he commanded attention. Ever since she'd known him he'd managed to combine physical beauty with easy grace, an innate elegance and a brilliant mind.

She'd loved his mind, and she wasn't going to think about his body—that had already kept her awake far too late last night.

Now she watched as he walked swiftly through the airport, shaking hands with several people he knew along the way. He was beautiful—ridiculous, movie star beautiful—with his thick onyx hair and incredible bone structure, and again whispers of conversation reached her, murmurs about news and weddings, and Jesslyn listened to the bits of gossip swirling through the terminal.

Was Sharif really thinking about getting married again? Was he close to taking a new bride? Had that decision already been made? And is that why he wanted her to work with his children this summer? To manage any problems the children might have before their problems became public?

Puzzled, she watched him reach the exit on the far side of the terminal. He hadn't once looked at her or for her, and she felt strangely numb, like a piece of office furniture.

But then he turned at the glass door, pushed up his sunglasses and looked straight at her with his startling eyes and that half smile of his that made her suck in air, dazzled despite herself.

So he'd known all along she was there, had been aware of her as he made his way through the terminal. Her heart did a painful little jump, an embarrassing little jump.

His eyes crinkled further, his mouth quirking higher, and he gestured to her, two fingers bending, calling her. *Come.*

Come.

If only he'd done that when she'd broken up with him. If only he'd called her, come after her, asked for her to return.

Sharif's men walked her to him now, and together she and Sharif stepped onto the tarmac, the June sun blisteringly hot despite it still being early in the morning.

"How are you?" he asked, as they climbed the stairs to the jet.

"Good," she answered, ducking her head as she entered the sleek jet. "How are you?"

He gave her a quick look, catching her tone. "Sounds like a loaded question."

She shrugged as they stepped into the jet. "People are talking about you."

"They always talk about me," he answered flatly, walking her to a chair in a cluster of four seats, two on each side of an aisle. Behind the seating area was a paneled wall with a handsome paneled door. "Which reminds me, I've a few calls to make. I'll be back out when we're airborne."

"Of course."

With a nod in her direction he disappeared through the paneled door. Jesslyn couldn't see what lay behind the door other than a room with pale plush carpet, the corner of a buttery leather couch or chair and lots of open space.

As the door closed, the flight attendant appeared at Jesslyn's side, checking to see if she needed anything. And then the door to the jet closed and within minutes they were taxiing down the long runway and lifting off.

Once at cruising altitude, the flight attendant returned, offering Jesslyn a choice of refreshments. "Tea, please," she answered, as Sharif reappeared, taking a seat opposite hers.

"Coffee, Your Highness?" the flight attendant asked.

"Yes, thank you," he said before looking at Jesslyn. "So what did you hear? What are the gossips saying about me today?"

She listened to the flight attendant's footsteps recede and looked at Sharif, really looked at him, seeing the fine lines fan from his eyes and the deeper grooves shaping his mouth. He looked pensive, even tired. Silently she debated whether she should even repeat the talk, if it was worth mentioning, but she'd heard the same talk twice now and it was better to know something like this than just wonder. "I heard you're to be married again."

His eyebrows lifted but he said nothing.

She watched his face. "Is it true?"

He hesitated a long moment. "There would be advantages to remarrying," he said at last. "And there are those who feel it would be advantageous for me to marry their daughter, but is there a bride? A wedding date?" He shrugged. "No. Nothing is set."

"But you will eventually marry?"

"I'm young. I'm a widower. It makes sense."

"It's just business, then."

He made a low, rough sound. "What would you prefer me to say? That I've met the most wonderful woman and I can't wait to marry my one true love?" He made the rough sound again. "I don't have time for love. I'm too busy running my country."

"How long have you been king now?"

Sharif frowned, trying to remember. "Five years? Six? Hard to recall. It's been long enough that it's starting to blur together."

"Your father had a heart attack."

"Died in his sleep."

"I remember reading it was a shock to the family. No one had expected it."

"That's what the media reported but it wasn't true. Father had problems several years before that, but his personal physician thought things were better. Mother hoped things were better. But I sensed that Father wasn't the same, but then, he hadn't been, not since my sisters' death."

Since the fourth form Jesslyn had loved his sisters, fraternal twins who had been completely different in every way and yet were still best friends, and over the years they'd become her best friends, too. Whatever Jamila and Aman did, wherever they went, Jesslyn could be found there, too.

After graduating from university Jamila and Aman had insisted Jesslyn come to live with them in London at the home of Sharif's aunt in Mayfair. Together they had dived into work, building their careers during the day and enjoying each other's company in the evenings. To celebrate finishing their first year as career girls, they planned a summer holiday in Greece.

They were on their last night on Crete when their car was broadsided by a drunk driver. Jamila died instantly, Aman was rushed to the emergency room, and Jesslyn, who'd been on the opposite side of the car, was hospitalized with injuries that hadn't appeared life threatening.

The hospital in Athens had been a nightmare. Jesslyn was desperate to see Aman but no one would let her into the intensive care ward since Jesslyn wasn't family.

Jesslyn remembered standing in her gown, leaning on her walker, sobbing for someone to let her in. She knew Jamila was gone. She was desperate to see Aman. It was then Sharif appeared and, learning what the commotion was about, he opened the door to Aman's room himself, firmly telling the hospital staff that Jesslyn was family, too.

That was how they met. In the hospital, the day before Aman died.

"I'm not surprised it affected your father so much," Jesslyn said, fingers knotting together. "I still can't believe they're gone. I think about Jamila and Aman all the time."

"The three of you practically grew up together."

She dug her nails into her palms, her throat aching with suppressed emotion. "Your parents blamed me for the accident, though."

"My father never did. He knew you weren't even at the wheel."

"But your mother…"

"My mother has found it difficult to accept that her only daughters are gone. But that's not your responsibility."

Jesslyn nodded and yet his words did little to ease her pain. The day of the funeral she wrote a long letter to King and Queen Fehr telling them how much she'd loved their daughters and how much she would miss them. The letter was never acknowledged.

A week after the funeral Jesslyn received a call from one of the queen's staff telling her she had to be out of the Mayfair house by the weekend because the house was being sold.

It was a scramble finding a new place to live on such short notice, but she did find a tiny studio flat in Notting Hill. Just days after moving into the new flat she collapsed. Apparently, she'd been bleeding internally ever since the accident.

The upside was they stopped the bleeding and did what they could to repair the damage.

The downside was that they warned her the scar tissue would probably make it impossible for her to ever have kids.

And then in the middle of so much sadness and darkness and loss, flowers appeared on her Notting Hill doorstep, white tulips and delicate purple orchids, with a card that said, "You can call me anytime. Sharif."

Sharif had scribbled his number on the card. She tried not to call. He was Prince Fehr, the eldest of the beautiful royal Fehr clan, the one Jamila and Aman had said would eventually inherit the throne.

But he'd also been kind to her, and he'd been the one to break the news to her that Aman had died.

Jesslyn called him. They talked for hours. Two days later he called her, inviting her out to dinner.

Sharif took her to a little Italian restaurant, one of those rustic hole-in-the-wall places with great food and friendly service. Jesslyn thought it was fantastic. Dinner was fantastic because it was so normal, so comfortable, with Sharif putting her immediately at ease. That night they talked about Jamila and Aman, they talked about Greece, they talked about the unseasonably cold weather they were having for late August, and at the end of the evening when he dropped her off, she knew she'd see him again.

She did see him again, she saw lots of him despite the fact that he was this famous rich gorgeous prince and she was, well, she was very much a nice, middle-class girl. But they enjoyed each other too much to think about their differences, so they just kept seeing each, never looking back, never looking forward. Not for two and a half years. Not until his mother found him a more suitable woman, a princess from Dubai.

"There are few people in this world like your sisters," Jesslyn said, her voice husky. "They were just so much fun, and so good humored." She tried to smile, but tears filled her eyes. "They knew how to live. They embraced it, you know?"

"I do know," he said as the hum of the jet changed and the nose dipped down. "Check your seat belt," he added gruffly. "We'll be on the ground soon."

A fleet of black Mercedeses waited at the airport, all in a line on the tarmac, not far from where the jet had parked.

In less than three minutes they disembarked, settled into the cars and were off, exiting the small private terminal reserved for the royal family's use and heading through the city streets to the palace.

Jesslyn already knew that Sarq was ninety percent Muslim and yet as they drove through the streets Jesslyn saw relatively few women wearing the veil, apart from a few still wrapped in white robes, and although she'd lived in the Emirates for the past six years, she was still surprised by how relaxed everything seemed, the people on the streets appearing open and friendly.

"It feels like everyone's on holiday here," she said, as the car idled at a traffic light waiting for it to turn.

"People say Sarq is becoming the southern Mediterranean's Costa del Sol."

"Is that good or bad?" she asked, watching a cluster of girls cross the street linked arm in arm.

"It depends on who you talk to. In the past ten years a rather staggering number of beach resorts—inexpensive as well as deluxe properties—have opened along the coast. Some welcome the growth with open arms—my brother Zayed—for one, while others, like my nomadic brother Khalid, want to ban further development."

"What do you think?"

"I'm in between. Economic stability enables Sarq to remain free and independent of any other country, and yet growth has a price. While the developing tourism industry has strengthened our economy, the environment's paid a stiff price with the destruction of sand dunes and the troubling disappearance of wildlife."

"You sound like you lean toward wildlife conservation," she said.

"I have to. My father didn't consider the impact development would have on our country's natural resources, and now I'm forced to deal with the consequences."

The car turned down a long drive marked by high stuccoed walls, lush, towering palm trees and flowering citrus trees beneath.

"We are here," Sharif added as the Mercedes sedan slowed

before immense wood and iron gates and the ten-foot-tall gates smoothly swung open.

Jesslyn craned her head to get her first look at the palace, a place she'd heard so much about from Jamila and Aman.

The girls had called the palace "heaven" and "paradise." They'd said it was like a jewel in the most beautiful garden ever, and indeed, as the car turned round a corner, she spotted a sprawling pink building, the palace a compound of one-story stuccoed villas draped with trailing purple, pink and peach bougainvillea.

Elaborately carved columns and miniature domes marked the entrance, and Jesslyn knew from her friends' description that inside were elaborate courtyards filled with fountains, dwarf palms and date palms and flowers.

White-robed and uniformed staff appeared in the entrance, greeting Sharif and welcoming the king home.

Sharif introduced Jesslyn, explaining that the teacher would be with them for the summer and he wanted everyone to make sure she lacked for nothing.

While Sharif communicated his wishes, Jesslyn surreptitiously glanced around. The palace's cool, crisp interior contrasted with the soft pastel hues of the exterior. The walls inside were white, the high ceilings painted blue and gold, huge carved wood columns soared up to support the elaborate ceilings forming cool narrow columned corridors and intimate seating areas.

Introductions finished, the staff dispersed and Sharif offered to take her on a minitour while they waited for his children to return.

"Where are they now?"

"Out for an afternoon excursion," he answered, "but they'll be back soon for tea."

Sharif's pride was tangible as he pointed out some of the rare works of art housed within the palace walls—paintings, sculptures, armor, weapons and more. Jesslyn was awed by the history of the collection, sculptures dating back to Greco-Roman civilization, a flawless mosaic from the tomb of a Byzantine king, an enormous scarlet rug that could be traced to the Ottoman Empire.

"And this has always been here?" she asked.

"For generations." He smiled faintly. "Some people go to museums to see priceless artifacts. I grew up with them, am still surrounded by them."

They'd reached the end of a long arched corridor, the stone floor patterned with sunlight shining through the dozen square windows high on the wall. The ceiling, painted shades of cream and gold, reflected the brilliant late-morning light and cast sparkly starbursts and circles on the whitewashed walls.

Before they'd even turned the corner, Jesslyn could hear the tinkling notes of a fountain, and indeed, as they walked through an arched doorway, they came to stone stairs that led to a sunken living room from which she could see the fountain in a picture-perfect courtyard.

"This must be where you entertain," she said, dazzled beyond words. The living room exuded elegance and beauty and calm, every detail exquisitely thought out, from the sweet spicy perfume of antique roses, to the huge glass doors drenched in sunlight, to the low cream couches that formed comfortable conversation areas.

"It's actually where you'll entertain," he said, an enigmatic smile lighting his eyes. "This is part of your room, the most public of your quarters."

She walked behind one of the sofas heaped with beaded and embroidered silk cushions in mouthwatering orange, lime and dusky rose. Impulsively she leaned over to touch one tangerine-colored pillow, and it gave beneath her hand, the down-filled insert deliciously soft.

"Oh, lovely," she whispered, unable to hide her delight. She'd lived such a Spartan existence these past six years, and the luxury here was beyond her comprehension. "This room is fit for a princess!"

"This was Jamila and Aman's room."

Straightening, Jesslyn turned to face him. "Really?"

He nodded.

Pain splintered inside her as she looked at the beautiful room and the fantasy courtyard with fresh eyes. "Maybe I shouldn't stay here."

"It'd be wrong for you not to stay here. My sisters loved you dearly. They'd want you here."

Blinking back tears, she drew a quick breath and ran a light hand over the tangerine pillow. "As long as it won't offend anyone. I don't want to offend anyone—"

"No one will be offended."

"If you're sure…?"

"You doubt me?"

She didn't know if she should laugh or cry and she did both, smiling unsteadily as she dashed away a tear. "I'm not normally this emotional and yet ever since yesterday I've been a disaster."

"It's a shock seeing each other," he answered.

Her head tilted and she looked up at him, her gaze searching his face. "You feel it, too?"

"How could I not? We were once very close. You knew me better than anyone."

A shiver coursed through her, a shiver of remembrance and hurt and pain. But she hadn't known him better than anyone.

His mother had known him better. His mother had known he'd choose his future, and his throne, over her.

Over love.

And he did.

Chilled, she turned, rubbed her arms. "Show me where the books are. I'm ready to look at everything, plan the afternoon's lessons."

"There won't be any teaching today. Use today to meet the children and settle in."

A knock sounded up the stairs on the outer door. "Ah, the children," Sharif said. "I believe they've arrived."

Instead Sharif's personal butler stepped into view at the top of the stairs. "Your Highness, an urgent call."

Sharif frowned. "The children aren't here?"

"No, Your Highness."

"They should have been here over an hour ago."

The butler paused, head bowing further. "I believe that is the nature of the phone call."

Sharif's expression didn't outwardly change, but Jesslyn felt a whisper of tension enter the room. "If you'll excuse me a moment," he said to her.

"Of course."

"This shouldn't take long," he added.

"Don't worry. Take as much time as you need. I can unpack."

"I'm sure that has already been done for you, but if you'd like to see your bedroom and ensuite bath, they are just through that door. In the meantime, I'll send for refreshment," he said as he started toward the stairs.

"I'm fine, Sharif. I can wait."

He turned in midstep, powerful shoulders shifting, robes swirling, his brilliant gaze locking on her face. "That's where we disagree," he said, his voice so rich, so beautifully pitched it pierced her chest, burying deep to beat in time with her heart. "I think we've waited long enough."

She didn't know if it was his expression or his tone of voice, but suddenly she couldn't breathe. "For tea?"

He paused, considered her, one eyebrow lifting. "If that makes you feel better."

CHAPTER FIVE

As HE LEFT to take the call, Sharif's thoughts lingered on Jesslyn.

She'd always been beautiful in that haunting English-beauty sort of way. A heart-shaped face framed by loose, dark curls. Flawless skin. Warm brown eyes. Perfectly arched eyebrows.

But there was something else different, something that he couldn't quite put his finger on but made him look and look again.

Beautiful yes, but more so.

Changed.

More reserved. Distant. Closed.

He'd watched her face, these past few days, as they'd spoken, and she'd treated him the way everyone now treated him—supremely politely. With deference, if not respect. And it didn't exactly bother him, but he missed the easiness between them. She'd always been the one person who had treated him like a man not a prince.

She'd teased him, laughed at him, loved him.

She'd loved him.

She didn't anymore. She hadn't when she'd left him nine years ago. And she hadn't when she'd begun accepting bribes from his mother.

But that was to come later. He'd get his answers later. In

the meantime he was determined to enjoy her beauty and revel in her softness and take what he could. Just as she'd once taken so freely from him.

After Sharif left to take the call Jesslyn anxiously paced the sunny living room with Sharif's parting words played endlessly in her head.

I think we've waited long enough.

What did he mean by that? What had they waited long enough for? And waited too long for what?

Was he referring to the girls? Was he wishing he'd taken action to help them sooner? Or…

Or…

She gulped a panicked breath, fingers squeezing into nervous fists. Was he referring to something far more personal, something that had to do with *them?*

Almost immediately she squelched the thought. Sharif had brought her here for his children. He wanted her for his children.

But still her heart raced and her body felt too warm and her veins full of fear and hope and adrenaline.

A soft musical sound in the doorway interrupted Jesslyn's pacing and turning. She watched a young, robed woman, a woman she guessed to be in her early twenties, descend the stairs carrying a heavy tray.

"Something for you, Teacher," the woman said in halting English as she carried the tray laden with food and flowers and a pot of tea into the living room.

Jesslyn felt some of her tension ease. "Thank you, that's lovely."

The woman smiled shyly as she placed the heavy silver tray on one corner of the low tables next to the cream-covered sofa. "I pour?" she asked, indicating the pot of tea.

There was something infinitely endearing about this young woman, and Jesslyn sat down on the couch. "What is your name?"

"Mehta, Teacher," she answered, kneeling and patting her chest and smiling again, this time revealing two deep dimples in her cheeks.

Jesslyn couldn't help smiling back. "Mehta, I am Jesslyn."

Her head bobbed. "Teacher Jesslyn."

"No, Jesslyn's fine."

She bobbed even more earnestly. "Teacher Jesslyn Fine."

Jesslyn liked Mehta, liked her a great deal. It couldn't be so bad here, not if she could see Mehta now and then. "Will I see you much, Mehta?"

"Yes, Teacher. I help you every day. With your clothes and bath and tea." She leaned forward, pointed to the tea. "I pour now?"

Jesslyn's cheeks ached from smiling. "Yes, please."

Along with the tea there were crescents of honey-soaked pastry stuffed with walnuts and pistachios, and the ever-popular *makroudi,* ground dates wrapped in semolina.

Jesslyn was shamelessly licking the sweet sticky honey from her fingers when Sharif reappeared. Mehta, spying Sharif, bowed and slipped soundlessly from the room.

In the meantime Jesslyn watched Sharif descend the pale stone stairs, and she could tell from his expression that he wasn't happy. His brow was dark and his jaw looked as though it'd been hammered from stone.

Sitting upright, she watched his progress across the floor of her lovely living room, troubled by the anger and frustration in his face.

It struck her that there was something else going on,

something he wasn't telling her, something he didn't want her to know.

She cocked her head, looked at him, trying to see past his striking good looks to what lay beneath. What was he really worried about? The girls failing academically, or the girls having emotional issues?

"It's the children, isn't it?" she asked

He nodded distractedly, his gray eyes burning with fire and frustration. "Yes."

"Are they hurt?"

"No. They're safe." He dropped onto the couch opposite hers, covered his face briefly with his palms and for a long moment said nothing, tension rippling through him in waves. He took a deep breath and then another before finally looking at her. "They're just not here."

"When will they be here?"

He didn't answer but she saw one hand curl, fingers forming a fist.

Did this happen often, she wondered, or was there something else troubling him, something more he hadn't told her?

"In time for dinner?" she persisted when he didn't answer.

He shook his head. "Hopefully tonight by bedtime, but realistically, it'll be tomorrow morning."

"Hopefully? Realistically? You're talking about your kids, right?"

Again his eyes flashed with frustration, but he didn't answer her directly, and his silence troubled her as much as the information he was telling her.

"Sharif, where *are* they?"

"With their grandmother."

"Zulima's mother?"

"Until recently Zulima's mother lived here, but she's returned to her family in Dubai. She lives with her second son now."

"So the children are with your mother."

He nodded.

Jesslyn was watching his face closely, trying to put the various puzzle pieces together. Sharif was leaving far more unsaid than said. "Why did Zulima's mother leave? Was there a problem?"

Sharif made a low mocking sound. "Is there ever not a problem here? The two mothers-in-law never did get along. It was always a battle of wills, and my mother tended to win."

His mother usually won, Jesslyn thought, more than a little concerned about what he was telling her.

Jesslyn knew Sharif's mother well enough to know that the queen had always been in charge. Sharif's late father might have been king, but Sharif's mother was the ruler of the palace.

Sharif's mother had never liked her. Not as Jamila and Aman's close friend. And definitely not as Sharif's girlfriend.

"So where are your mother and the children right now?" she persisted.

"She has a small house on the coast, about an hour and fifteen minutes north from here. It used to be the summer house where we'd go for holidays, but my mother has claimed it for herself." He reached across to the table, checked to see if she had any hot water left in the pot. There was none and he let the lid fall. Meanwhile his expression grew blacker. "She took the girls there this morning and they're with her now."

"Did she not know you'd be returning today?" she asked, thinking that it was going to be hard enough living in the palace without having to contend with Her Highness, Queen Reyna Fehr. Her Highness had actually grown up as a commoner in the Emirates but had made up for her lack of royal connections with stunning cheekbones, a perfect nose and best of all, a very rich father.

"She knew," he answered tautly. "We talked last night and again this morning. But she does what she wants when she wants and everyone else can be damned."

Jesslyn bunched an iridescent pillow and held it to her chest. "You and the girls see her often then?"

"Every day. She might have claimed the summer house but this is where she still lives, this is home. She just goes to the summer house when she wants to make a point."

Jesslyn was having a hard time taking in everything Sharif was telling her. Queen Reyna had never wanted Jesslyn to be friends with her daughters and she'd made that clear in a hundred different ways over the years, but this, this was a relationship between a doting mother and her eldest son. "And what is the point your mother is trying to make?"

Sharif made a rough, mocking sound. "That she's in charge."

Things were starting to become clearer. "Does Her Highness know I am going to be working with the girls for the summer?" she asked.

He paused, and that hesitation alone gave Jesslyn her answer.

Sighing, Jesslyn sank back against the low couch and clutching the pillow even tighter, closed her eyes. "She doesn't know."

"She knows I was bringing back a tutor."

She opened her eyes and gave him a pained look. Sharif was in fine denial mode today, wasn't he?

And maybe, just maybe, this denial mode wasn't helping the children adjust to their school or their life without their mother.

But before she could find a delicate way to say any of this, Mehta returned with another tray. "Tea, Your Highness," she said bowing low before Sharif and placing the tray on a table in front of him.

"Mehta, I can pour for His Highness," Jesslyn said, drawing the tray closer to her so it wouldn't be in Sharif's way.

"Yes, Teacher Jesslyn Fine," Mehta answered with yet another bob of her head before hurrying away.

Sharif glanced at Jesslyn. "Teacher Jesslyn Fine?"

Jesslyn grimaced. "I think she believes Fine is my last name."

Sharif just looked at her a long moment before shaking his head. "You're an interesting woman."

"A euphemism for an odd, peculiar spinster?"

"We know you're not a spinster," he flashed, watching her fill his cup. "You've had boyfriends."

"I have," she said after a moment. "And it seems you have your mother."

Sharif's head jerked up and he nearly spilled his tea. "What?"

"You said your mother wants to think she's in charge, and I'm curious to know, is she?"

Sharif gave her a withering look. "No."

He might say no, she thought, but if Queen Reyna thought she was, or could be, you had the makings of a classic power struggle, the kind she'd seen between parents many times before, but in this case, the struggle was between father and grandmother. "Are you and your mother disagreeing on how to raise the girls?"

He barked a laugh, ran his hand through his dark hair, his expression tortured. "Not that I know of."

"Then what?"

He lifted his hands in mute frustration. "There's something wrong here, but I don't understand it. I don't see the children enough to know how they really are. When we are together, they hardly look at me or speak to me. When I ask them a question they do answer, but they stare at the floor the entire time and—" He sighed. "I've never known children to behave this way. My sisters certainly didn't behave this way. I'm confused."

"So what is it that you really want me to do, Sharif? Teach the children? Be a companion to them? Observe their behavior? What?"

He looked up at her, gray eyes shot with bright silver, and yet there was no light in his eyes right now. "All of the above."

"So essentially you want a nanny."

"No, they have a nanny. I need…" His voice drifted off and his forehead creased. "I need you."

She wasn't sure what he meant by that, but there was something in his eyes, something in his expression that made her heart ache. Impulsively she reached out toward him. She'd meant it to be a friendly touch, warm and reassuring, but instead of touching the loose sleeve of his robe, her fingers grazed his forearm, his bronzed skin warm like the sun, and she shuddered, stunned by the electric heat.

Abruptly she pulled back, pressing her hand to her breastbone. She'd imagined that fire, she told herself, she'd imagined that wild streak of sensation that had raced up her arm, into her shoulder, into her chest. But looking into Sharif's eyes she suddenly wasn't so sure.

There was the same fire in his eyes, a fire that made her remember how it'd been in his arms, beneath his body, in his bed.

"Something wrong?" he asked, his gaze traveling slowly over her hot face.

Fresh heat surged through her cheeks making her skin sensitive and her lips tingly. "No," she breathed, nervously pressing her hands to her lap. "I just think it'll be good when your daughters get here. It sounds as though there is much work to do."

"You will be very busy," he agreed, his gaze now resting

on her mouth as if fascinated by the curve and color of her lips. "Perhaps you should welcome having the rest of the afternoon and night free. Once the girls return you won't have much time to yourself."

She felt her lower lip begin to throb as though it had taken on a life of its own. It was all she could do not to cover her mouth. "I just wish it was sooner rather than later. It's still early in the day and I know you have work to do—"

"I'm sure Mehta would be delighted to show you the library. It's where you'll be teaching tomorrow. Feel free to have a look around and examine some of the books I've bought."

"That's an excellent suggestion. I'll use the afternoon to begin preparing tomorrow's lessons. Thank you."

Rising to his feet he smiled vaguely, amused by her enthusiasm. "So you'll be fine on your own this afternoon?"

"Yes. Definitely."

"Great. I'll see you at dinner—"

"Maybe we should pass on dinner," she suggested hurriedly, unintentionally interrupting him. "I'll have tons of reading to do tonight and I know you've a great deal of work."

He stared down at her, and she had to tilt her head back to see him.

"We'll talk about the children during dinner," he said blandly. "That should make you feel better." He started to leave but paused on the stairs. "And dinner, Jesslyn, is always at seven."

The afternoon passed far too quickly for Jesslyn. She'd discovered the library and had immediately fallen in love. The room was huge and airy, a beautiful gold dome topping high walls lined with floor-to-ceiling shelves. The library reminded Jesslyn of some people's ballrooms, large enough to comfortably hold two couches, two wooden desks, four armchairs and a long antique table with impressively carved legs.

She found the stack of teacher's editions right away, but before sitting down with those, she looked at the books the children were using. She was familiar with the publisher, and had taught the middle school version of the literature and language books. The material she'd be teaching was simple enough. Her concern was the quantity. There were stacks of books for each child. Math, science, social studies, literature, grammar, foreign language, and then music and art books, too.

Jesslyn carried the stack of children's books to one of the armchairs and sitting down with notepad and pen, she looked at the number of chapters in each book, and then the number of days between now and school starting, and mapped out a plan of how much could be comfortably covered in each subject.

She was still hard at work four hours later when Mehta lightly knocked on the door. "Ready for a bath, Teacher Fine?" she asked with her dimpled smile.

Jesslyn glanced up quizzically. "A bath?"

"Before dinner."

"Ah. Right." Closing the science textbook she wondered how to explain to Mehta that she didn't feel it necessary to take a bath before dinner. She'd taken a shower that morning and it was just a business dinner. "I have so much to do before tomorrow that I might just wash my face and touch up my hair for dinner."

Mehta looked at her uncomprehendingly. "No bath?"

"I took one earlier."

"No bath before dinner?"

Jesslyn set the book down. "I don't take a bath before every meal, Mehta."

"No bath."

"No."

Mehta's dark brows pulled. "No dinner?"

"No, I will have dinner. I'm meeting Sheikh Fehr for dinner at seven. We are meeting to discuss business—"

"Dinner with His Highness."

"Right." Jesslyn smiled with relief. Finally. They were both on the same page. "Dinner," she said. "At seven."

Mehta held up her wrist, tapped her wrist as though there was a watch there. "Half past five. Dinner seven. Bath now."

Jesslyn sighed heavily. She really didn't want to argue about a bath with a young member of Sharif's palace staff. She'd only just arrived and she was going to be here all summer. And from the sound of things she was going to need someone on her side.

"A bath sounds lovely," she answered with forced cheer as she reluctantly moved all the books off her lap and chair so she could stand. "But I'm not finished with these," she added. "I'll want to read them later."

Mehta was delighted. "Yes, Teacher Fine. Now come."

Jesslyn hadn't seen the bedroom before, but following Mehta down the columned hall into the bedroom, she discovered that the bedroom with its spacious antique bed was just as lovely, and even more feminine, than the sunken living room.

The antique bed reminded Jesslyn of a Russian ballet with dramatic floor-to-ceiling pink and rose silk and satin curtains that could be untied and draped around the bed to provide intimacy and seclusion. The bed, built like an oversize daybed, had neither headboard nor footboard but high sides softened with pillows to match the silk panels.

A short silver vase teeming with fragrant pink rosebuds sat on a side table, and Jesslyn bent over to breathe in the heady sweet perfume. It wasn't easy to grow roses in the blistering heat of the desert, which made these all the more precious.

"Your bath," Mehta said, standing in yet another doorway gesturing to a room beyond.

The bath was a Roman bath with sunken tub and endless white marble. A delicately painted dome arched over the airy room, capping high walls with high narrow windows that drew in early-morning and late-afternoon sun but didn't sacrifice privacy.

"I will help you?" Mehta asked, gesturing to Jesslyn.

The huge sunken tub had already been filled, and steam rose from the surface. "I can manage," Jesslyn answered, thinking the whole help thing had gone far enough. Turning, she spotted a white robe on a small iron stool, and she picked it up, held it against her. "I'll take the bath and then put this on and then I'll come out, okay?"

Mehta smiled. "Okay."

Once the bathroom door was shut, Jesslyn dropped her clothes and slid into the tub's hot water with an appreciative sigh. She hadn't wanted to take the bath, but now that she was here, chin-deep in water scented with a tantalizing vanilla and spice oil, she couldn't imagine not bathing.

The little bathroom in her apartment had a tiny tub, but the water never got properly hot and then turned cold halfway before the tub was even filled. Soaking in this deep tub was pure decadence. Closing her eyes, Jesslyn just floated, content, absolutely content—

"Massage now, Teacher Fine. Okay?"

Mehta's voice suddenly pierced Jesslyn's dream state and her eyes flew open. Mehta was leaning over the tub smiling at her. "Okay?"

Jesslyn sat up abruptly, drawing her knees to her chest. "I don't need a massage."

"Nice massage before dinner."

Spotting a large woman, Jesslyn shook her head. "The bath is perfect. The bath is lovely. I'll just get dressed."

"Dinner with His Highness," Mehta said.

"Yes, yes, I know, but—"

"Massage before dinner with His Highness."

Oh, for Pete's sake! Enough with this dinner-with-His-Highness. It was just Sharif. She'd had hundreds of meals with Sharif. It was ridiculous to go through all of this just because she'd be joining him to eat.

"No." Jesslyn hugged her knees tighter. "I really—" she broke off as the masseuse behind Mehta scooped up the robe and came marching toward her.

Mehta and the masseuse waited expectantly.

Jesslyn looked up at them, water trickling down her chest and back. She honestly didn't know if she should laugh or cry. Coming here, she thought Sharif would be the problem, but Sharif was no problem, not compared to her baby-faced attendant with the biggest dimpled smile in the world.

"Anything for the king," she said from between gritted teeth as she stood up in the bath and was wrapped in the robe.

Mehta smiled, her deep dimples growing bigger, deeper.

But of course Mehta smiled. Mehta was having a great time. She'd managed in less than a day to turn Jesslyn into a living Barbie doll.

CHAPTER SIX

JESSLYN'S heart thudded as she stood in the doorway of the royal courtyard. She couldn't take another step, painfully self-conscious in the open-shoulder silk blouse Mehta had insisted she wear after going through all of Jesslyn's clothes. The black silk was sheer and heavily embroidered with silver, the top draping off her shoulders and then dipping low.

It was a splurge top she'd bought for the Australia trip, a dressy fun top she'd imagined wearing in Cairns or Port Douglas for a special dinner out. Instead she wore it tonight for dinner with Sharif, the top paired with slim black satin trousers and high heels.

"Where did Miss Heaton go?" Sharif's deep voice sounded from the opposite end of the courtyard, and Jesslyn searched the shadowy walled garden lit only by moonlight and the odd torch.

"I'm not sure," she answered nervously, taking another step into the courtyard, feeling the chunky, black wood bead necklace sliding across her bare skin. "This wasn't my idea," she added defensively, pressing the big glossy wood beads to her sternum, wishing the beads covered more of her as her top left far too much bare. She shouldn't have allowed Mehta to dress her. She should have finally, firmly, put her foot down.

Sharif moved from the shadows into the light. "I've never seen you like this."

Instead of his traditional robes, he wore Western clothes, tailored black trousers and a long-sleeved white dress shirt open at the throat.

She'd never seen him like this, either. In London they'd never dressed up, never gone to very expensive or trendy restaurants. Instead their lives were simple and low-key and yet so full of happiness.

"This isn't my idea of business attire," she added nervously, shoulders lifting at the warm caress of the evening breeze. "But Mehta doesn't listen to me. Not about anything."

"Ah, yes, Teacher Fine," he remarked moving leisurely toward her as the torches jumped and flickered in the breeze. "And you do look very fine."

She touched one bare shoulder, aware that her top's black silk was so sheer her skin and the curve of her breast could be seen. The fact that the silk had been bordered in silver ribbon and embroidered with fanciful silver designs did little to comfort her. The top had merely seemed playful when she'd planned to wear it on holiday. Now it felt far too daring, provocative and sexual and it mortified her.

She wasn't trying to seduce Sharif. She wasn't trying to do anything but fulfill her promise to him. All she wanted to do was help his children and then return to Sharjah in eight weeks for the new school year.

"Would you like a cocktail, a glass of wine or champagne?" he asked.

She fidgeted with the black beads. "No, thank you. I don't really drink. I know a lot of the expats in the Emirates do, but since most people don't drink…" Her voice trailed off as she looked up into his face, her train of thought disappearing as she got lost in his eyes, eyes that tonight looked like the pewter gray of the precious Tahitian pearl.

"How is life in Sharjah as an expat?" he asked, his head tilting to one side, his lips curving lazily, and yet the cool, sardonic smile only made the spark in his eyes hotter.

"Good. I'm happy there. It's become my home." She tried to smile, but found it impossible when Sharif was looking at her like that.

Looking at her as though she was the most interesting thing in the world.

But she knew what she was and she knew what she wasn't, and this—all of this—was a huge mistake. She should never have come to dinner dressed this way.

A lock of her dark hair fell forward, and reaching up, she shyly pushed it back from her brow. Mehta had done her hair, as well, brushing and backcombing the crown, before sweeping most of it away from her face and pinning it at the back of her head with small jeweled hairpins that left some hair loose in soft dark curls.

Looking in the mirror at her reflection earlier, Jesslyn had nearly fainted. It wasn't that she didn't look beautiful, but the hairstyle and the blouse and the dark eyeliner and pale glossy lips all whispered sex. Seduction. Pleasure.

She'd tried to take the jeweled hairpins out, but Mehta had shocked her by bursting into tears. "No Teacher Fine, no," she'd wept and Jesslyn had been so stunned and so uncomfortable she'd left her hair and makeup alone.

Jesslyn tried to smile but couldn't quite pull it off. "Sharif, I really feel awkward. This outfit, this hair—" She lifted a hand, gesturing to her head, hating how her hand shook like a nervous schoolgirl's. "This isn't me. It isn't right. I'm sorry."

"Don't apologize, that's really not necessary. But I do agree with you. Something's not right." Sharif folded his arms across his chest, his features firming in lines of concentration as he slowly walked around her, studying her from head to toe.

Then, turning away, he called a quiet command and one of Sharif's uniformed butlers appeared. Sharif spoke quickly, two or three abrupt sentences that Jesslyn couldn't follow. She spoke basic Arabic, but he wasn't speaking a dialect she understood.

She looked at Sharif questioningly as the butler disappeared. Sharif simply looked at her, his expression unreadable. "This shall be an interesting evening," he said at length, allowing himself the smallest hint of a smile.

His smile filled her with fresh trepidation. She didn't want an interesting evening. She wanted a safe evening, a predictable evening, an evening that was courteous, professional, routine. The Sharif standing before her at the moment represented none of those things.

"I spent the afternoon reading through the children's textbooks," she said with unintentional force. She was nervous, so nervous, and already she felt wound too tight. "I'm quite familiar with the publisher as I've taught the middle school editions of the literature and language books, and as textbooks go, they're very good."

His silver gaze gleamed. Deep grooves bracketed his sensual mouth. "I'm glad you approve."

She had to look away, unnerved by the intensity of his gaze. He was looking at her far too intently, looking at her as though he could strip her bare at any moment, as though he would strip her bare at any moment....

"The science and math textbooks are of course new to me. I'm not credentialed in those subjects, but it's not difficult material to teach." She was babbling, knew she was, but couldn't help it. Anything to keep from thinking about his eyes, his mouth, his lips. Anything to keep from looking at the width of his chest and the beautiful bronze skin revealed by his open shirt. A shirt like that wouldn't be acceptable in his culture, but he didn't seem to care about rules.

Regulations.

Propriety.

"I'll work with them on handwriting, too," she added breathlessly. "I imagine Takia is still just learning to print."

He didn't answer and she glanced up, looking at him from beneath her mascara-coated lashes. His jaw flexed. He was fighting a smile. She knew because she saw the briefest flash of his white teeth.

"Are you afraid to be alone with me?" he asked, an eyebrow half rising.

"No." She laughed and it came out high and thin, more like a hysterical bleat. "No," she repeated more firmly. "I'm just thinking about the children. Our first day of school."

"You're a most dedicated teacher."

She refused to meet his gaze and she stared at her fingers and the ring on her right hand. "I try."

"I like that about you." He paused expectantly as the butler returned with a stack of medium to large jeweler's boxes. "Let me see what we have."

Jesslyn watched as the butler opened one box after the other for Sharif. A priceless necklace nestled inside each box's black velvet and satin lining, thick diamond clusters, long strands of large black and white pearls, a glittering sapphire, diamond and South Sea pearl necklace.

She'd never seen jewelry like this, never in her life. She'd seen photographs in magazines of exquisite jewels, had watched a famous actress claim an award with borrowed

Harry Winston diamonds, but that was on TV and everyone knew television wasn't real life.

As each box opened Sharif glanced at Jesslyn, his gaze narrowed consideringly. After the third and final box opened he turned to her, "Which do you prefer?"

Heat stormed her cheeks. "Don't tease."

He shrugged. "I'll pick the necklace for you, then." And after perusing the selection for another minute, he lifted the dazzling, thick, diamond necklace, an entire strand of diamond starburst after diamond starburst, and moved behind her.

"Lift your hair," he said.

"This is absurd, Sharif."

"Your hair."

A shiver raced down her back as she hesitantly reached up to take off her wood bead necklace and to pull her heavy hair off her neck, revealing her bare nape and nearly naked back.

She closed her eyes as she felt him settle the heavy necklace around her neck, his fingers brushing her skin as he deftly fastened the small hook. The necklace was cold against her chest, hitting four inches below her throat.

"Turn. Let me see," he said.

Slowly she turned to face him and he took a step back to give her a critical once-over. "Pretty," he said, but he didn't sound very convincing, and yet with so many huge diamonds she knew the necklace had to be worth hundreds of thousands of dollars. If not more.

"Please take it off," she urged, looking down and catching sight of the diamonds' white fire.

Instead he turned to another jewelry box, the one with the decadently long strand of flawless South Sea and Tahitian pearls, each pewter and cream-colored pearl the size of her knuckle. Unhooking the clasp, he lifted the pearls from its box and, again moving behind her, he draped these around her neck. The pearls fell between her breasts, hung so low that the luxurious strand brushed the full swell of her breast before settling low against her breastbone.

"Turn," Sharif commanded.

She gave him a fierce look over her shoulder. "Remember our conversation from last night? I am your employee, not your servant."

He met her angry gaze and he smiled slowly, a provocative gleam that quickened her pulse and turned her belly inside out. He was playing a game, a game she didn't understand, a game where he made the rules and she was to follow.

"What do you want?" she whispered, her voice failing her.

"I want to see you covered in jewels, the way you could have been." His lashes dropped, concealing the pearl gray of his eyes. "The way you would have been."

Goose bumps covered her arms. The fine hair at her neck stood on end.

"You could have been my queen," he repeated.

She looked at him, seeing him as the world must see him, that noble face both beautiful and severe, and then there were those eyes of his, those silver eyes that had haunted her in her sleep for years.

She'd told herself after leaving him that she'd never regretted ending their relationship, told herself she was better off without his controlling mother and foreign culture and far-off palace, but at night her dreams told her differently.

At night, even years later, she still dreamed of him, and in her dreams she tried to cling to him, tried to make the differences go away. Tried to redeem herself.

Now she reached up to try to remove one of the necklaces, but before she could unfasten a clasp Sharif gently batted her fingers away and, taking the diamond, sapphire and pearl strand from his butler, he told her to lift her hair.

She shook her head. "I can't do this anymore."

"But you still have one more."

"No. I don't want it, I don't want any of these."

"But you like jewelry. You love fine jewelry. And best of all, you look stunning in exquisite jewels like these. Now lift your hair because dinner is being served and we don't want it cold."

She looked up at him, bemused. She'd never owned fine jewelry, only trinkets and hand-me-down bracelets and necklaces and rings from her mother. An antique cameo. A silver Art Deco brooch. Wooden bangles. A jade pendant.

"I don't feel comfortable, Sharif."

"But you look beautiful. You're absolutely gorgeous. Like a living treasure."

He was paying her compliments and yet there was an edge to his voice, an unspoken anger.

"Maybe we should just eat," she whispered.

"One last gift," he said. "Please move your hair."

Eyes burning, she gathered her heavy hair into her hands and lifted it high to give him access to the back of her neck. His fingers brushed her skin, his fingertips so light, so teasing she arched helplessly at his touch.

She didn't want him.

But she did want him.

She didn't love him anymore.

But she loved the way his skin felt on hers, loved the heat and how he made her feel so hot, so electric.

She wanted more heat, more hot, more electric. Closing her eyes she could imagine his hands on her hips, his hard body against the back of her thighs, his palms sliding up her ribs to cup her breasts.

Then suddenly his lips were there at the back of her neck, planting a fleeting kiss where his fingers had been.

"There," he said, his voice deep, warm reminding her of honey and sun. "Perfection."

Turning her around, he extended her a hand. "Dinner, *laeela*."

They were eating outside at the opposite end of the courtyard, dinner served in a beautiful pale-ivory tent lit by a delicate crystal chandelier hanging above the linen-covered table. Three more white candles flickered on the table, making the porcelain china shimmer. Tuberoses and white lilies floated in water, their fragrance so sweet it nearly made her dizzy.

Or maybe she was dizzy because Sharif watched her so intently she felt as though she couldn't breathe properly.

Dinner started with a variety of appetizers, ranging from roasted peppers with feta and capers to artichoke hearts with ginger, honey and lemon, followed by chilled almond and garlic soup with roasted chili and grapes, then course after course including spiced *kefta*, lamb meatballs, poached in a buttery ginger and lemon sauce, beef *tagine* with sweet potatoes, spicy beef *koftas* with chickpea puree.

The parade of dishes didn't stop until the very end when they were presented with a choice of desserts, figs and pears in honey or Sharif's favorite, *m'hanncha*, crisp buttery filo filled with an almond paste, spiced with cinnamon and scented with orange flower water.

Jesslyn refused dessert, too full, too nervous, and too anxious to leave. She wanted the meal to end, but Sharif ordered one of each dessert and strong coffee.

After the steward left, Sharif leaned back in his chair. "You said Sharjah feels like home. But how did you end up living in the Emirates? It seems like a most unlikely place for you to settle."

Jesslyn shifted in her chair and as she did, the low pearl necklace unexpectedly swung between her breasts, brushing one breast and then the other, and the touch of warm pearls on her skin felt strangely erotic.

She squeezed her thighs tighter, not wanting to be distracted by sex, and yet the pressure only made her more conscious that she was aroused.

"When I was teaching in London at the American School I heard there was an opening at the American School in Dubai. The pay was very good and I was getting bored in London, felt restless. I thought I'd go to Dubai for a year, teach, have a bit of adventure and then return." She shrugged. "I never returned."

"How long did you teach in Dubai before taking the job in Sharjah?"

"I was there only a year, but the private school in Sharjah suited me better. Smaller school, more hands on, I could help decide the curriculum. I like that."

What she wasn't telling him was that Germany and France both had faculty openings in their American schools but she chose Dubai because she missed her friends, she missed Jamila, Aman, and…Sharif.

How could she tell him that living and teaching in the Emirates made her feel as though she were still somehow close to all of them? That living as an expat in the UAE felt more comfortable than living anywhere else?

"But you'd never even visited the Emirates before," he persisted.

"I know. But I've never stopped missing your sisters," she said. "Living in the Emirates I can almost imagine that I'll run into them again. You know, turn a corner, and there Jamila will be, her eyes sparkling with laughter, a huge shopping bag on her arm.

"Jamila loved to shop," Jesslyn continued, feeling the words rush through her nearly as intense as the emotions. "And of course Aman liked nice things but not like Jamila. I remember one time Aman shouting she'd never ever go out with Jamila again because all Jamila ever did was shop, shop, shop…" Her voice faded and she lifted her shoulders.

"I know you're getting tired of hearing this, but I really do miss them. They were both so fiery and fun, so full of life. I've never been able to replace them. But then, I've never wanted to."

"I could never get tired of hearing you talk about them. No one else speaks about them." His brow furrowed, and he looked at her for a moment as though puzzled. "You really did love them."

"Of course I did. They were my best friends. But you know that." Looking at his face, she suddenly wasn't sure that he did. "Sharif, you've always known your sisters were my closest friends."

"It's hard to know sometimes what's real. What's true. And what's fiction." His gaze narrowed and he stared past her, his expression inscrutable. "I've learned in the past nine years that things aren't always what they seem."

She clasped her hands in her lap. "Like what?"

It seemed as though he was going to answer, and then he shook his head. "But it's good to hear you talk about my sisters. My mother doesn't mention them anymore. I don't think anyone does."

"You don't, either?"

"I should, but I haven't. So many years have passed, and their deaths created so much pain that I suppose we've all tried to move on, forget."

The back of her eyes burned hot and gritty, and she blinked

to keep the salty sting from blinding her. "I don't want to forget them. I like thinking about them. They were so loving, so warm."

He glanced from one of the flickering torches back to her. "They were loving, and protective of those they loved. And especially protective of you."

Jesslyn heard that hint of anger in his voice again, as though there was something he very much wanted to say but couldn't or wouldn't. And yet it made no sense. Why would Sharif be upset with her all these years? He was the one that married quickly. He was the one that had a family and children. She was still single, still trying to come to grips with love in all its different forms.

They were still sitting in silence when their attendant returned with coffee and dessert. Jesslyn took her coffee and added several teaspoons of sugar.

"Your brother, Khalid," she said awkwardly, trying to move the conversation along, "he doesn't speak of the girls, either? If I recall, he was quite close to them. I know he took their deaths very hard."

"I don't know who took it worse—Khalid, my father or my mother—but it has been very difficult for Khalid. He was three years younger than the girls, and my sisters absolutely doted on him. Khalid worries us sometimes, he's quite the loner. We don't see much of him. I haven't seen him in at least a year."

"Where does he live?"

"The middle of the Great Sarq Desert." He exhaled wearily, rubbed his brow. "He's our nomad. A scholar, a gentleman and a recluse, but also unreachable—" He broke off, shrugged impatiently. "But what's the expression, 'We can't save everyone?' I suppose we're lucky if we can even save ourselves."

"Sharif, are you angry with me?"

"Why would you think that?"

She didn't know, couldn't imagine. He'd married the woman he'd wanted to marry. He'd had the life he wanted to have.

Hadn't he?

Reaching out he touched the diamond necklace glittering against her skin and then trailed his finger to the second strand, the pearl and diamond and sapphire one, and then down lower to the warm pearls nestled between her breasts.

She inhaled hard, a quick silent protest as the back of his fingers brushed her breast slowly, so slowly she knew he was aware of what he was doing.

"I never could see you here," he said, stroking beneath the heavy pearls, caressing the vee between her breasts and then over to the other side to brush the full swell, her nipples now erect, pressing brazenly against the sheer fabric of her silk blouse. "You were always so smart and kind and sweet. You were open and sunny and fun. But you were a bit scruffy in your jumpers and corduroy skirts and jeans. You're not scruffy anymore. You're stunning. Otherworldly."

The entire time he talked, he touched her, fingers tracing maddening circles on the sides of her breasts, and she did nothing to stop him. Nothing. Because she wanted that touch, as improper as it was. She wanted him to run his hands along her rib cage beneath her breasts. She wanted him to take her aching nipples in his fingers, in his teeth and suck and lick and kiss and bite.

She wanted his hands on her body, on her belly, on her hips and between her legs.

She wanted him poised between her thighs and she wanted to feel him again, feel him press into her, his shaft hard, thick, hot.

And she never thought this, wanted this, with her previous

boyfriend, Robert. She never thought this, wanted this, with anyone but Sharif.

But Sharif wasn't interested in her. He was just toying with her, punishing her.

With effort she pulled away. "You made the right woman your queen," she said, reaching up to remove the first necklace, the diamond starbursts, and drop it in his hand, the brilliant stones catching the candlelight and casting long glittering rays in every direction. "Your mother approved. Your father approved. You made everyone happy."

His fingers closed around the diamonds. "Even you?"

Ah, that one hurts, she thought, taking a short, sharp breath as she worked at the clasp holding the sapphire and diamond necklace around her neck.

Did he know that too late she realized she'd martyred herself, rejecting him in a fit of childishness and then too proud to go to him and say she was wrong, she'd been wrong, she'd just been acting out.

Looking back at how she'd been, she realized now she'd been not merely young, but naive. She'd actually thought Sharif would come after her, she'd thought he'd declare his undying love and devotion and they'd marry and live happily ever after.

Ouch. Talk about living in a fantasy world. Finally the clasp opened, and drawing the diamond and sapphire necklace from her neck she draped it across his wrist.

"Were you happy with my decision?" he persisted.

"I don't know how to answer that," she answered trying to smile, because truly, she wouldn't have been a proper wife for him, she wouldn't have served him or the country, not the way she was. But she had loved him, as passionately and completely as she could love anyone.

Leaning forward, he wiped a finger beneath her lower lashes. "A tear," he said, holding his finger up for her to see and a small opalescent tear trembled there.

"There are always regrets, Sharif." And she smiled harder, smiling against the tears as she began to unhook the clasp of the pearl necklace. "But here we are, nine years later, and so life is full of surprises, little twists and turns we never see coming." And then she sniffed, battling to hold back the tears. "I can't undo the necklace. Would you please unfasten it for me? I never thought we'd speak again."

"Keep it," he said, his gaze holding hers, the silver depths enigmatic. "Another souvenir for your collection." And then abruptly he leaned forward, covered her mouth with his and kissed her.

It wasn't a tentative kiss, no shyness involved. He kissed her hard, parting her lips beneath his and plundering her mouth with his tongue. It was almost as though he was taking her mouth the way he would take her. Hard, fierce, mercilessly.

Just as abruptly he broke the kiss off. "Consider this necklace paid for."

He was gone, walking away before she understood he was finished and leaving.

Confused, she sat and watched him go, and it wasn't until he was gone she numbly realized he'd never touched the desserts, nor his coffee, and she'd only had that one sip of hers.

He was angry with her. Very angry. And she didn't understand why, how or what. But she just realized that what he wanted from her might have nothing to do with the children.

CHAPTER SEVEN

On his roof terrace, Sharif leaned against the cool wall, robe hanging open over his trousers, and stared up into the moonlit, star-drenched sky.

He knew better than any that two wrongs don't make a right and yet he'd intentionally seduced Jesslyn tonight, starting with the bath and then the massage with the scented oil. He'd told Mehta he wanted Jesslyn to wear beautiful clothes, and Mehta had answered that Jesslyn had no beautiful clothes, just ugly teacher things.

However, in the end, Mehta had found something sexy, far sexier than anything he could have imagined Jesslyn wearing, and things had progressed from there.

But he wouldn't call tonight a success.

He didn't know who he'd upset more tonight—her, or him. Because he was upset. He was troubled. Angry. Guilty. Obsessed.

Obsessed with kissing her. Touching her. Feeling her body against his.

Digging his knuckles into the wall, Sharif knew he wasn't just obsessed with possessing her. He was obsessed with the need to come to grips with his life, including the past he'd lost, the present that tormented him, the future he couldn't have.

By bringing her here he'd thought he'd finally get some answers, find some peace, but her presence was having just the opposite effect.

She'd thrown him straight back into hell.

So much for killing two birds with one stone. Jesslyn might be able to sort his children out, but she was torturing him.

All these years he'd been angry with her for betraying him. All these years he'd imagined her living it up in Dubai, living a lavish lifestyle supported by his mother, and yet on visiting her school and then her apartment he found she lived like a pauper.

So where was all the money his mother had given her?

What had she done with the treasured family jewels?

Had she spent all the money?

Or had she needed the money for something he didn't know about? Had she been pregnant? *What?*

The what was driving him half mad.

But he'd get the truth, he told himself, forcing a deep breath, struggling to relax. And the best way to get the truth was to stay with the plan. Perhaps the plan was cruel, but as he'd told her last night in Dubai, he needed the truth.

After all these years, after a painful marriage, after his wife's tragic death, Sharif wanted—craved—truth.

He didn't even have to like it. He just had to know it.

But that kiss tonight…that kiss had nearly dismantled him. How could the kiss of a woman break you?

Again he clenched the wall, his heart blistered all over again.

He'd loved her endlessly once. He couldn't have imagined life without her. How much would he have sacrificed for her? What would he have risked?

Everything.

Everything.

* * *

Jesslyn was up early, before it was fully light. Dressing quietly, she washed her face, pulled her hair into a ponytail and headed to the library.

The palace was dark in places while in other areas she saw lights and could hear voices as the palace staff prepared for another day.

Nodding to various security staff, she entered the library, gently closed the door and turned on the light. Her books were where she'd left them and, returning to the armchair, she curled up and set out to finish what she'd started yesterday— a schedule for the summer.

There was no way to cover everything, but she'd spend the first week doing informal assessments, discovering what the girls knew and didn't know, before diving into half-day lessons followed by afternoons free for play.

She was still hunched over the books, taking notes, scribbling plans when the door opened. She'd expected Mehta and coffee, but it was Sharif, and immediately her insides buzzed with butterflies. He'd changed so, he wasn't even the Sharif she knew anymore, and she wasn't sure how to cope.

"Good morning," she said, hiding her unease.

"I was told you've been in here working since five-thirty," he said.

"I couldn't sleep. Wanted to get the rest of the lessons mapped out."

"You're very dedicated."

"You're a concerned father and I've promised to do what I can."

He nodded, glanced around the room and then back to her. "Have you had coffee or breakfast yet?"

"No, but I'll get some coffee soon. I'm beginning to drag a bit."

Sharif reached for the door. "I'll have them send some to you. And toast?"

"Toast would be lovely. Thank you."

He paused. "I heard from my staff that you're having difficulty reaching Robert on your wireless phone. If you'd like to use the house phone, you're more than welcome."

"Thank you," she answered awkwardly. The truth was, she hadn't tried very hard to reach Robert. She'd pulled her phone out twice, and left him a message once, but he'd never called her back and she'd given up. Temporarily, of course.

Fortunately, toast and coffee arrived. Unfortunately, it arrived with Sharif. He didn't take a seat, though, just stood inside the doorway while the breakfast tray was set up near her armchair. "Is there anything else you need? Fruit? Water?"

She clutched Jinan's science book to her chest. "No, this is great. I'm set."

She'd thought he'd leave then, but he didn't. Instead he watched her, his brow furrowed, creases fanning from his eyes. He seemed perplexed by her, which was perplexing in and of itself. They'd never had a complicated relationship. Having met under such horrible circumstances, they'd been open from the start.

"I was thinking about something you asked me yesterday," he said unexpectedly. "You wanted to know if my daughters took after my sisters, and this morning it hit me that Saba, my middle daughter, is the most like them. Saba's my feisty one. I thought middle children were supposed to be the peacemakers but she has some of Jamila's boldness."

"So she'll be my little fighter," Jesslyn said, smiling.

Sharif suddenly smiled back. "Takia would be the lover."

"And she's the youngest."

He nodded. "My little one."

"And your eldest daughter?" she asked.

"She's a typical firstborn. Smart, responsible, hardworking. A perfectionist, and a little mother to Takia."

"But aren't Jinan and Takia just a couple of years apart?"

"Two and a half."

"Amazing." Jesslyn shook her head, unable to imagine having three children in as many years. "Your wife was amazing. I couldn't do that, have so many children so close together."

Sharif tipped his head against the wall. "Neither could she," he hesitated, remembering. "She died after complications from an emergency C-section."

"After Takia's birth?"

"No. After the fourth baby. The baby was stillborn."

Jesslyn shuddered inwardly. What a terrible loss for the entire family, both mother and baby dying and then leaving three small children behind. "I'm sorry."

"She didn't give her body a chance to recover between pregnancies. After each baby she wanted to try again. And again." His jaw jutted grimly. "It was madness. It—" He broke off, swallowed hard. "It killed her."

Jesslyn had always felt such jealousy whenever she'd thought of Sharif's beautiful noble wife. Just seeing Princess Zulima's photograph in a magazine used to fill her with the worst sort of pain. But that jealousy changed now into something else entirely. Sorrow. Pity. "But why did she rush so? You were both young. You had time, and it's not as if you didn't have children. You had those little girls."

But the moment the words were spoken she knew. Lifting her head, she looked into Sharif's eyes.

Little girls.

And what was it that Queen Reyna had said to her all those years ago?

Sharif needs sons if he is to be king. Sharif needs heirs who will inherit the throne from him.

And you, Queen Reyna Fehr had said, *looking straight into Jesslyn's troubled gaze, can't have children. Can you?*

"Despite all that, you were happy with Princess Zulima, weren't you?" she asked quietly, her fingers gripping the book tightly. "You never regretted marrying her."

His dark brows pulled. "Is that a question or a statement?"

She grinned. "I'm not sure. Maybe both." She looked at him, and then as she stared at him, taking him in, her smile slowly faded.

The years had changed his face so much, adding deep lines and worry and shadows to his beautiful eyes. She missed his easy laugh. She missed his warmth. She'd once loved him so much it grieved her to see him this way.

"If I have regrets," he said carefully, "it's that we came here to the palace to live after we married. We would have been better off living abroad, or getting our own home."

"It was difficult for her here?"

He shrugged almost tiredly. "It was difficult for both of us, but she never complained."

Just like his children, she thought, biting her lower lip. "She sounds like a lovely person. Incredibly brave. I would like to have known her."

Sharif laughed roughly and ran a hand through his dark hair, combing it back from his face. "No, you wouldn't. Zulima was beautiful, well educated and royal. But she wasn't very friendly. She didn't have time for people who weren't…"

"Royal?" she supplied when he seemed to struggle to find the right word.

"Important," he corrected mockingly. "In that respect she and my mother were cut from the same cloth."

"So your mother and Princess Zulima were friends?"

Sharif barked a laugh. "Zulima hated my mother."

"Was your mother meddlesome?"

"My mother wasn't a real royal." His expression turned sardonic, and he folded his arms over his chest, the simplicity of his white robe a perfect contrast to his chiseled features. "Living here was like walking on eggshells. Someone was always upset. Lots of drama, lots of tension." His voice dropped low, so low that his next words were all but inaudible. "I hated living here. Everyone did."

Jesslyn wasn't sure she'd heard him correctly and she didn't know what to say. Platitudes at this point were just that, platitudes, and pointless. "Perhaps your children still feel sadness here. Perhaps this palace reminds them too much of what they lost?"

"Then wouldn't they be happy in England? Wouldn't they want to stay at school?" His head shook, his expression dark, brooding. "You'll see once the children arrive what I'm talking about. The girls don't laugh or giggle. They barely talk, and when they do, it's just with each other."

No, not normal, Jesslyn thought, not for three girls that age. "What about affection?" she asked. "Where do they go for hugs? Comfort? When they have nightmares or scrape a knee?"

"Their nanny tries," he answered flatly.

"What about you? Don't they want to come to you?"

Again that odd haunted look came into his eyes. "No."

"Why not? You're not an ogre. You talk about them with such love—"

"Talk's cheap though, right?" Abruptly he pushed off the wall, glanced behind him, down the column-lined corridor. "They're here," he said, the shadows deepening in his eyes. "They've arrived."

* * *

Introductions were even more strained and painful than Jesslyn had imagined. The girls stood before their father in the palace's soaring entrance, with shoulders straight and heads bowed. They never once looked up at him. For his part, his voice was without warmth or emotion.

"My daughters," he said, pointing to each child in turn. "Jinan, the eldest. Saba, the middle daughter. And Takia, the youngest."

Each child bobbed a head, but none looked up and none greeted her with words or even a curious glance.

Jesslyn knew Sharif was watching her face, trying to read her reaction. Thank God she could hide her emotion behind professional detachment because frankly, she was shocked. These children resembled beautiful wooden dolls. He'd been right when he said there was no life in them, no sparkling eyes or quick smile.

If children had come to her classroom like this, she would have immediately suspected abuse. Whether it was hunger, deprivation, emotional neglect or physical abuse she wouldn't have known right away. Just as she didn't know the source of *their* misery yet. But she would.

Looking down on their small dark heads, she vowed she would. If not for Sharif's sake, then the children, because Jamila and Aman would never have stood for this. Never. Jamila and Aman's nieces deserved better.

A half hour later Jesslyn ushered the girls into her sunken living room, which now streamed with warm white-gold sunlight.

She had her small charges sit on the floor in a circle among the big silk pillows, and she took a seat with them. Sitting like this, on the floor, eye to eye, she could see their faces better, and the children were absolutely beautiful, perfect oval faces with high regal brows, elegant winged eyebrows, large eyes, small straight noses and little rosebud mouths. With beauty like this, they'd be models or child actresses in any other culture.

"We're going to play a game," Jesslyn said cheerfully, knowing that all she'd be doing the next few days was trying to crack that wall they kept around them, and trust didn't come overnight. It'd take time, but it'd be worth it. These children needed to laugh. They needed to smile.

"Do you have a favorite game?"

The girls just stared at her.

"Well, I play lots of games," she continued brightly, "and I wanted to teach you one of my favorites. It's called Duck, Duck, Goose."

The girls' expressions turned even more wooden if such a thing were possible.

"I'll go first and I'll show you how to play." Jesslyn got to her feet. "I'm going to go around behind you and I will tap each of your heads and say duck, duck, duck, until I finally say goose and when I say goose, whoever gets 'goose' jumps up and chases me."

"Why would we want to chase you?" Saba blurted, and all three girls stared at Jesslyn, waiting for an answer.

Jesslyn shrugged. "Because it's fun to jump up and down and run around." She could see from their cloudy eyes she hadn't convinced them of anything. "You'll see once we get going."

Little Takia's brow furrowed. "And why is it goose? Why isn't it chicken?"

"Excuse me," Jinan cut in imperiously, "but *Jaddah*, Grandmother, said we were to be studying. Why aren't we doing maths and reading books?"

Jesslyn had to fight to keep a straight face as she gazed into their pensive little faces. "You'd rather do maths than run around and play?"

"Playing is for children," said Saba.

Jesslyn bit down on the inside of her lip to keep her smile from showing. "I believe your father told me you're five, six and seven years old."

"Actually, Jinan turned eight last week, and I'll be seven in two months," Saba said, a flicker of disdain in her eyes.

"How lovely, did you have a party?" Jesslyn asked, turning toward Jinan, the most grown-up eight-year-old Jesslyn had ever come across in her life.

Jinan shook her head.

"Why not?" Jesslyn asked.

"Parties are for little children," Jinan informed Jesslyn.

"Ah, I see," Jesslyn said, thinking that there were already quite a few things she'd like to say to Sharif, but knowing she'd have to wait until later when the girls returned to their nanny for free time.

"What do you see?" Takia asked, sounding confused.

"I just see the bigger picture now," Jesslyn explained. "I see why you don't want to do games and run around and play. You're all older now and you're thinking about university, and where you're going to go and what you're going to do—"

"I don't want to go to university," Takia interrupted with a wail. "I hate school."

"We all hate it," Saba chimed. "And we hate going to England but we have to do it."

"But sometimes England is better than here," Jinan said meaningfully, looking at her two sisters.

Interesting, Jesslyn thought, sitting back down on the floor and rejoining the circle. "When is boarding school ever better than home?"

But suddenly the girls were all tight-lipped again, and they just looked at her with their big serious eyes and their small pinched lips, lips that looked as though they were hiding some very heavy secrets and stories.

"Well," Jesslyn said. "I guess we're going to play some games. I'll go first. And the game is played like this," and she launched into a demonstration that soon had at least Takia in a fit of giggles.

Outside the living room Sharif stood in the hall listening to Jesslyn convince the girls that her game was fun, and he wasn't sure she could succeed until he heard Takia's peal of laughter.

Her laughter made his chest ache.

He hadn't heard that sound in so long.

What had happened to them all? What had happened to his children? What had happened to him?

He didn't know, although he'd tried talking to the children's headmistress. He'd even switched the girls' nanny here. But nothing had made a difference. The girls wouldn't speak to him unless it was a formal good-morning or good-night.

But Jesslyn would help. Jesslyn had already helped, he told himself, heading toward the entrance where his limousine waited.

He was stepping into the limousine when his mother appeared. "You're leaving without saying hello or goodbye?" she asked coldly, standing so stiffly before him that her veils slid over her shoulder revealing her dark hair without a hint of gray

Sharif's jaw flexed. "You don't take my children out of the city without my permission."

"I just took them to the summer house."

"Listen closely. If you ever take my children from the palace without permission again you'll not be allowed back here. Is that clear?"

His mother's eyes glittered with humiliation. "You've no right to speak to me that way!"

Sharif smiled thinly. "I've every right when you publicly shame me—"

"I've never."

"Every one of my staff knows you were not to have taken the children for the day. Every one of my staff knows you were to have been here for tea yesterday, and instead you spend the night at the summer house."

"The traffic—"

"We have our own helicopter, remember?"

She gestured impatiently. "If you're so upset, why leave now?"

He didn't immediately answer, battling to keep his temper in check. "You knew I had to fly out to Paris this morning. You knew I only had yesterday with the children."

"It's impossible to keep track of your travel schedule."

"I'll have a calendar made for you." And putting his hand on the door he stepped into the back of the car.

She walked closer. "Make one for the children, too. I'm afraid your daughters don't even know you."

He looked up at her, and a dozen protests came to mind, a dozen things he could say in his self-defense. But she was right. His children didn't know him. Today they hadn't even looked at him when he greeted them in the hall. They'd stared at the ground as though he were their worst nightmare.

Pain burst through his chest, red and hot and endless. My God, how did a life that started so promising, become a nightmare like this? "I'll be back on the weekend. Let the children know they can call me anytime."

She lifted her chin. "You can call them."

His burning gaze met hers. "Mother, I try. But someone has to locate them and then put them on the phone."

* * *

Late that afternoon Jesslyn walked the girls to their wing of the palace where their nanny, Mrs. Frishman, waited for them. Jesslyn's first impression of Mrs. Frishman wasn't that positive. The older woman, hired for the summer, seemed far too dour for such young children, but Jesslyn secretly hoped this was just a first impression and her feelings would change upon getting to know the Swiss German nanny better.

"I'll see you at dinner," Jesslyn said as Mrs. Frishman appeared in the doorway. "I'll be interested in hearing how you spent the rest of your afternoon—"

"The children have dinner with their grandmother," Mrs. Frishman interrupted sharply.

"Very nice," Jesslyn answered. The children glanced up at her, their expressions uneasy, and their unease just fed her own. What were they not telling her? she wondered. What was it the girls wanted to say, but wouldn't?

Clearly they weren't comfortable enough to speak candidly to her yet, and so she reached out, touched each child on the top of the head. "Perhaps I'll come say good-night to you once you're in bed."

"It is my job to put them to bed," Mrs. Frishman said, large hands folded in front of her. "You are the teacher. I am their nanny."

Jesslyn's outward serenity never slipped. "Excellent. Then you girls are free of me for the night. But I will see you in the morning after breakfast and be prepared for lots of work then."

"Right," Takia said. "Like Duck, Duck, Goose."

Jesslyn could feel Mrs. Frishman's disapproval and she hid her smile. "Exactly. More Duck, Duck, Goose, and other difficult endeavors." And lifting her fingers to her lips, she blew them a kiss. "Until tomorrow, then."

Turning away, Jesslyn walked back down the hall, conscious that four sets of eyes watched her go, and while she was no mind reader, she could have sworn that the children didn't want her to leave.

Returning to her own wing, Jesslyn walked through her living room and then out the large glass door to her sun-drenched courtyard. Potted lemon trees were interspersed with tree roses, and Jesslyn wandered through the fragrant garden, sniffing blossoms, admiring the vivid apricot- and coral-hued roses. Yet as much as she appreciated the beautiful garden, she couldn't shake her apprehension.

What had traumatized the children so? What was making them withdrawn and fearful in their own home?

"Teacher Fine," Mehta called to her from the doorway. "Would you like tea now?"

"Yes, please," Jesslyn answered gratefully, "and could I enjoy my tea out here? It's lovely in the garden now." And it was lovely with the high walls creating a welcome shade and the twitter of birds mingling with the sound of the splashing fountain.

Mehta returned a few minutes later and presented her with an enormous black binder.

"I'm sorry, the tea isn't ready," she said, bowing. "But His Highness said to give this to you. You are to use it."

Jesslyn watched Mehta hurry away, then glanced down at the big bulky binder in her lap.

What was this? Information from the school? Medical records? Copies of the children's transcripts and homework?

Curiously Jesslyn opened the binder and scanned the table of contents and realized with a start that the binder wasn't background information on the children, but information for her about her job.

The binder was organized in such detail that there even was a table of contents and four separate sections. As she leafed through the binder she saw that every section dictated how she was to behave here, and how she was to interact with the children.

There was to be no hugging, touching or other inappropriate interaction.

The children were to use quiet voices at all times. There was to be no laughing, no singing, no games.

No laughing? No games?

Jesslyn's brow creased and she continued reading, increasingly troubled.

The girls were not allowed to watch television unless it was educational, and even then, only proper programs celebrating their Sarq culture.

The girls were to practice restraint. Tantrums, tears, theatrics and other displays of inappropriate emotion were never permitted.

By now Jesslyn could hardly keep reading. Her chest hurt. Her heart raced. She felt absolutely sick to her stomach.

Swallowing the acid taste in her mouth, she forced herself to move on to Education & Objectives. Surely this wouldn't be so severe, and indeed, this section was relatively basic. The girls were to study every day, to cover all sections in their textbooks that they had received low marks in, and to improve their study skills tremendously. But in addition to eight hours of study a day, they were expected to take twice-weekly dance lessons and voice lessons, they were also required to get thirty minutes of "other" rigorous exercise daily, as well as practice piano and violin an hour every afternoon, and that didn't include art lessons, either.

Swiftly she added up the number of hours to be spent in the classroom, then hours in exercise, hours performing arts, hours practicing one skill or another and the children's day was endless. It began early, concluded late and, studying the list of activities, Jesslyn saw no time scheduled for just old-fashioned play. There was no free time at all, no opportunity for little girls to jump rope, play with dolls, play dress-up or play house.

Everything was regimented. Everything scheduled to the minute.

Little wonder the girls were depressed. Jesslyn felt depressed just looking at their schedule. Taking a pen from her purse, she began making notes in the margins.

She was so busy reading the pages, snorting at the ridiculous expectations and making notes in the margins that she didn't realize someone was standing at her elbow, reading over her shoulder until she heard a very cold female voice.

"You have a problem with your responsibilities already, Miss Jesslyn Heaton?"

Jesslyn startled, jerking upright, hating the shiver that raced through her. She'd know that voice anywhere. Queen Reyna Fehr. "I'm just not sure what this is," she answered, lifting the binder.

"It's obvious. It's your resource binder." Reyna leaned over and snatched the black binder with both hands. "And you're completely defacing it."

Jesslyn felt heat rush through her cheeks, but she held the elder woman's gaze. She wasn't twenty-something anymore. She wouldn't be intimidated. "Well, I won't be using that book, so you can keep it."

Reyna's stare only grew more withering. "It's for you. It explains exactly how to do your job here."

"Thank you, but I don't need to be told how to do my job." Jesslyn stood up so she could be eye level with the queen. "I've already mapped out a course of action for the summer—"

"But this is what we've been using all summer, and this is what you will also follow."

"No," she said quietly.

Reyna's jaw dropped. "Pardon me?"

"No, Your Highness." Jesslyn saw the astonishment on the other woman's face and she felt a tiny prick of pleasure before squashing it. She wasn't here to pick fights or even win them. She was here to help Sharif's children. "The children are seriously depressed. I've rarely met such unhappy little girls, and that binder is partially to blame."

"How can you say that? The children are floundering academically—"

"Only Takia is floundering. I looked at the headmistress's letter. And Takia's floundering because she's homesick. She's far too young to start school—"

"Enough," Queen Reyna snapped, cutting her short. "You don't even know them. You've only just met them. You're in no position to take that tone with me."

Years ago this would have crushed Jesslyn, but nine years ago she didn't know how ruthless or manipulative Sharif's mother could be. "Maybe I don't know them yet, Your Highness, but I make my living working with children and I know how to teach them. And I will teach them, but I shall do it my way."

"I will speak to Sharif!"

"I wish you would," Jesslyn answered evenly. "And while you're at it, do let him know I'll be speaking with him, too."

CHAPTER EIGHT

JESSLYN waited all evening to be summoned to Sharif's chambers. She remained dressed so she'd be ready to go the moment he was free. She'd sent two messages with Mehta, and then one with Sharif's personal butler.

But Sharif didn't call for her, and at midnight, her stomach in knots, Jesslyn finally went to bed.

The next morning she discovered why she'd never heard from Sharif. He was gone, away to Paris, and wouldn't be home for five days.

It would have been nice for him to tell her.

She spent the next few days busy assessing the children's strengths and skills, while introducing the first of the lessons. The children were very bright and enjoyed learning, and as she praised them for their excellent reading and writing, they positively blossomed, somber faces beginning to offer shy smiles.

Counting the days, Jesslyn knew Sharif should be home tomorrow. There were so many things she needed to discuss with him. But the next morning she was informed by Queen Reyna that Sharif would only be home for a brief visit before flying out early the next morning and wouldn't have time to see her.

"He'll see the children," Jesslyn said, trying to hide her disappointment.

"Of course. But they're his family."

Jesslyn sent word to Sharif's butler, anyway, that she needed to see the sheikh when he returned home. She told him it was about the sheikh's children, and the butler assured her he'd pass the message on.

But once again she didn't hear from Sharif, not that night nor the next morning.

Not about to give up, Jesslyn sent another message later in the day that she had to see His Highness, that it was absolutely essential and urgent that they meet. She had concerns about the girls, questions to ask, things only he as the children's father could answer.

This time he sent word back that he'd very much like to meet with her but he'd already left for Jordan, and from there he'd head to New York. However, once he was back in Sarq he'd definitely sit down with her and listen to her concerns.

Her concerns, she thought, sitting at the library table with the children and looking at their bent heads as they labored over their math problems.

Her concerns were his concerns. Her concerns were his children.

A half hour later when the girls had finished their math, Jesslyn casually asked the children if they'd seen their father. "Were you able to see your father while he was home?"

Jinan stacked her books. "He came to say good-night to us last night."

"Did he read you a story?" Jesslyn asked.

Saba's lips pursed. "He doesn't read."

Jinan frowned at her sister. "He reads," she corrected, "but he doesn't read to us."

Jesslyn leaned on the table, arms folded. "But it was a nice visit, right? You talked. You told him about your day and your studies…?"

The girls just shook their heads.

"Why not?" Jesslyn persisted.

"We can't bother him," Takia said.

Jesslyn looked from one to the other. "Why not?"

The girls struggled to answer but finally Saba just shrugged. "*Jaddah,* Grandmother, says he has many worries and we must not trouble him."

Jesslyn reached out and covered Saba's hand with her own. "But it's not a trouble for him to hear about your day. Your father wants to hear about your day."

The girls looked at each other and then Jinan shook her head. "We can't bother him," she repeated stubbornly. "He's the king."

Jesslyn swallowed hard, forced a smile and vowed to speak to Sharif the moment he returned, no matter the cost. She would see him and she would make him understand that it was Sharif who had to change. It was Sharif who had to fix things.

Fortunately, the next five days passed with surprising speed, and by the end of the second week the little girls' shy smiles had turned into giggles and bright eyes. The girls had taken to holding her hand as they walked through the palace gardens. Takia was skipping. Jinan and Saba were telling her jokes. Thirteen days and the girls were finally acting the way little girls should.

Friday arrived, the Friday when Sharif was to return again. She knew he was to return between ten o'clock and midnight.

All evening Jesslyn kept an eye on the clock, and when ten o'clock arrived, she left her room and, ignoring Mehta's anxious enquiries about where she was going, headed to the wing that housed Sharif's personal chambers.

Sharif's butler must have been informed she was coming

as he met her midway down the hall to tell her that His Highness had not yet returned.

Jesslyn looked at the butler for a long moment. "I must see him."

"But he is not yet here."

"He is coming home tonight though."

The butler inclined his head. "Yes, but he could arrive very late. I will tell His Highness that you wish to speak to him and tomorrow you can—"

"I'm not waiting for tomorrow," she said, interrupting him as politely as possible. "I will stay up and wait for him here."

The butler looked aghast. "You cannot wait here."

"Why not?"

He glanced around. "There's nowhere to sit."

"I'll stand."

"But you can't. It's not proper."

"Why not?

The butler was completely flummoxed. He looked over his shoulder, to the left and then the right before throwing up his hands in a helpless gesture. Jesslyn actually felt rather sorry for him.

"I must see His Highness." She smiled apologetically. "And I'm going to stay here until he comes home."

The poor man gave her a rigid half bow before stalking off only to return minutes later with a small stool and pillow.

"Here," he said gruffly. "You must at least be more comfortable."

Jesslyn smiled her thanks and sat down on the stool next to the wall. She wasn't sure how long she'd wait, but suspected it could take a while.

And it did. Fifteen minutes became thirty, thirty minutes became an hour.

An hour.

Jesslyn sighed and tried not to fidget, but she was getting numb from sitting on the small stool even with the pillow. There were plenty of things she wanted to do, needed to do, but right now nothing seemed more important than speaking with Sharif about his children. So she'd wait.

Leaning back against the wall, she bent her legs and tried to relax, telling herself it couldn't be long now. It was nearing midnight. Surely Sharif would arrive soon.

Another half hour passed, creeping by with exhausting slowness. Her head felt heavy, her eyes gritty. She'd close her eyes just for a moment, just to relax for a moment.

"What are you doing here?"

It was Sharif's deep voice speaking from very far away. Jesslyn sleepily opened her eyes and as she opened them she realized where she was, and how she was right now sitting on the marble floor at Sharif's feet.

"Waiting for you," she answered, blinking up at him as she unsuccessfully hid a yawn. "They said you were coming home tonight and I had to talk to you."

"It's nearly three in the morning."

"Oh. It is late." Jesslyn tried to get up, discovered one foot was asleep and with a yelp, sat back down. "Just a minute. It's got that pins-and-needles feeling."

"You've been here since when?" he asked, gazing down at her, his expression somewhere between pity and shock.

She yawned again, finding it very hard to wake up. "Um, ten, tenish."

"Five hours," he muttered. "Unbelievable."

"I insisted," she answered. "You never called me this week and I left you so many messages."

His hands were on his hips and he just shook his head at

her. "Unbelievable," he repeated before crouching next to her and scooping her into his arms.

She stiffened instinctively. "What are you doing?"

He stood easily, lifting her as though she were a child Takia's size instead of a woman. "Taking you back to your room."

He'd already set off for her room, walking swiftly through the halls, his stride long. Her heart beat hard and fast. She felt silly, vulnerable, shy. This was an intimacy she couldn't handle. "Put me down, Sharif," she whispered into his neck as they passed members of Sharif's security detail, "this is embarrassing."

He grimaced. "Imagine how I felt finding you sleeping on the floor outside my chambers."

"I wasn't on the floor. I had a small stool," she protested, wiggling her legs and trying to slide free. "I can walk now. My foot is awake."

He didn't let her go. "We're almost there."

He was right. They'd reached the stairs to her living room and he carried her down those, across the spacious room to the adjoining bedroom.

"All right, I'm here," she said, as he entered the bedroom. "You can put me down now."

Sharif lowered her onto the bed and then took a step back. "No more waiting up half the night to see me."

She looked up at him. "I wouldn't have to wait up if you'd just return my calls."

He stared down into her eyes, his own gaze troubled. "I'm sorry. I never got the messages."

"I asked on four different occasions, spoke to three different household members and palace staff letting them know I needed to speak to you."

Deep furrows etched across his brow while fine lines

deepened at his eyes. He seemed to struggle to find the right words. "Things here at the palace are not what they should be."

"That's a fact."

She got up onto her knees to better see his face. "Things are absurd here, Sharif. You say you want what's best for your daughters and yet—" She broke off, her courage suddenly flagging.

It was one thing to understand a problem; it was another to voice it. In Sarq, men were responsible for taking care of their women, including their mothers. Mothers returned to their sons' homes after their husbands died. Mothers were protected, cherished and supported by their sons. Sharif was the eldest of the Fehr brothers. It was his duty, his responsibility, to provide for Reyna, but in this case the personal cost was too high.

"Yet what?" he pressed.

"It's nearly four in the morning. This isn't the time."

"It's nearly four in the morning. We're running out of time." He put a finger beneath her chin, tilted her face up to his. "So tell me, you've been here nearly two weeks on your own. What's wrong with my children?"

She scanned his face, searched his eyes. How was she to say this? How could she put it without stepping on his toes? "That binder you left for me, the one full of a hundred horrible rules—"

"What binder?"

"The black one, the one that says your children can't be hugged, touched or kissed. The one that says they can't laugh or tease. The one that insists they must study ten to twelve hours a day. That binder."

"I don't know what you're talking about. I never left you a binder. I would never make up, or enforce, rules like that.

Surely, you know me better than that. It must have come from my mother."

If he thought this would soothe her, he was wrong. She reared back, balled her hands on her thighs. "That doesn't strike you as wrong? As deeply, morally offensive? Your mother has created a virtual prison for your children and you shrug it off with an 'Oh, that's my mom.'"

"That's not what I said!"

"No, but it's damn close." She was breathing hard, her pulse racing. "The problem isn't your children. It's your mother."

"I get your point," he said flatly.

"You don't. You've no idea. Your mother is filling the children's heads with fears and phobias that have no bearing in reality."

He sighed wearily. "I know you've never liked her—"

"That's not what this is about! It's about protecting your children!"

"From my mother?" He gave her an incredulous look. "Jesslyn, you forget I am her son and this is her home, too."

"I know you're her son, and I'm aware this is her home, too, but maybe you need a home of your own." She reached out to tug on his robe, wanting him to listen, really listen and not just give lip service to her words. "A home where *you* are the head of the household, and the father to your children, a home where you can make the decisions without constantly being challenged."

He pushed one of her dark curls back from her cheek. "And you wonder why my mother didn't take to you all those years ago."

"I was always nice to her. Too nice," she added faintly, closing her eyes at the feel of his fingers. Every time he touched her she thought her heart would burst. Every time he came near she wanted that past they'd shared, they'd lost.

"Can we just forget about my mother for a moment?" he asked, thumbs sliding beneath her jaw to clasp her face.

"But we can't forget her. We—you—have to do something about her."

"I will." And then his head dipped and his mouth covered hers in a kiss so slow, so sensual she had to grasp his robe with both hands for support.

Part of her brain was telling her there was no way she should be doing this again. Part of her brain was telling her she had to stop, had to pull away, but another part of her brain was drugged, seduced by the hot, sweet pleasure of his mouth on hers and his warm strong hands on her skin.

He nipped at her lower lip with his teeth before exploring the same tender lip with his tongue. Shivering, she leaned against him, and Sharif wrapped an arm around her, drawing her even closer to his muscular frame, holding her so firmly against his powerful body that every breath he took teased her nipples, every flick of his tongue made her more aware of his erection pressing urgently against her hips.

The pressure was a bittersweet pleasure, stirring fresh desire, a purely wanton need.

She'd forgotten that a man's body could feel like this, had forgotten the sinewy pressure of a man's thighs and the width of a real chest. She'd forgotten that bodies could feel so good so close together, and while she'd had several other relationships in the past nine years, it'd never been like this. Never this heady, dizzy seduction of memory and emotion and the senses. And until now she hadn't realized how closely desire was tied to emotion, because she didn't just want him physically, she wanted him the way she'd once wanted him—mind, body and soul. She didn't just want his fingers and lips and skin, she wanted his heart, too.

They were both nearly out of control, a fact she registered in the dimmest part of her brain, but instead of putting a stop to the passionate frenzy, the thought had the opposite effect, driving her to frantically slide her hand beneath his robe, wanting his bare chest, wanting to find that heart she'd lost years ago.

Kissing her even more deeply, he lifted her off her knees and onto her back, before stretching out over her.

She shuddered as he lay on her, his body so warm and powerful and hard, and it hit her yet again how much she'd missed him, how much she'd missed this. Almost whimpering, she tried to drag his robe off so she could feel him properly against her. Skin to skin. Chest to breast.

As she pushed at his robe, struggling to get it off his thickly muscled shoulders, he unfastened the buttons of her navy knit blouse until the blouse lay open in a puddle of fabric at her sides.

Lifting his head, he gazed down at her, gray eyes dark with passion, and he looked at her as though he'd never seen her before, looked at her as though he might never see her again. The expression in his eyes was enough to make her chest constrict and to cut off the air in her throat.

Eyes burning, she slid her fingers through his dark hair, fingers twining tightly in the crisp, silken strands, dragging his head down, dragging his mouth back to hers.

This time she kissed him, this time she kissed him hard, fiercely, opening her mouth to him, playing with his tongue, sucking on the tip to try to drive him wild, wanting him to feel what he was doing to her.

What he'd always done to her.

She loved him. She hated him. She was half-dead without him.

Tears slid from beneath her lashes as she gave herself to him, overwhelmed by the hunger and the need and the knowledge that this, what they were doing now, would never happen again.

Sharif's hands were everywhere, on her belly, on the cleft between her thighs. He was touching, stroking, making her soft and wet, so wet that she had to have him, with her, in her.

She helped push his trousers over his hips and then leaned over his body to kiss the flat hard muscles of his abdomen and the smooth arc of hipbone and the lean line of muscle of his thighs.

As she kissed down his thigh, her lips and tongue alternating soft kisses with flicks of her tongue, she felt his hands bury in her hair, tugging at her head with the urgency of his passion.

She knew what he wanted, and felt his hands on her breasts, cupping the fullness of her breasts as she bent over him, her mouth now so close to his rigid shaft but still not giving him the satisfaction he ached for.

Sharif massaged then pinched her nipples between his fingers, his body straining, his skin hot, glowing golden. She blew warm air across the tip of his erection, heard him groan deep in his throat and then lightly, so lightly she took the head of him into her mouth.

He was huge in her mouth, and yet so beautifully firm and warm and satin smooth, his thickness perfect for his length and with her hands and mouth she stroked him until, panting, he abruptly pulled her off.

"I don't want to know who taught you that," he growled, voice raspy, his eyes burning with hunger, fire.

She stared into his eyes, wanting to remember this, wanting to remember him, wanting to have all the passion she'd gone without for the past nine years.

"You did," she whispered, lightly raking her nails down his chest, savoring the texture of his skin over hard muscle.

"We never did that before."

"I always wanted to. So tonight I did."

He lifted her off her bottom and onto his thighs, forcing her to straddle him. "Why?" he asked huskily.

Her shoulders lifted and fell. "I wanted to see what it'd be like if you were mine."

She heard his swift intake of breath, felt his hand bunch tightly in her hair, and after staring up at her for long, silent minutes he released her hair and his hands slid down over her shoulders to the fullness of her bare breasts.

"Has it always been this way with us?" he asked, a strange note in his voice.

She had to swallow against the tears. "I don't know. I don't remember." *I just remember how much I loved you.*

"I want you. Heaven knows I want you, even though I don't know what that means—"

She cut him off by leaning forward and covering his mouth with hers, kissing him slowly, softly, kissing him with her eyes closed so that he couldn't see how much she needed this, wanted this, wanted him. She wasn't experienced in bed, the only time she'd ever enjoyed making love had been with Sharif, but after all these years she knew what their bodies were for and she knew what making love meant.

And kissing him, she took away all the words, all the thoughts, all reason. Kissing him, she took away everything but the moment because that's all she wanted. She never asked for anything for herself. She never wanted anything for herself, but right now she wanted this. She wanted him.

One night. Right now.

But Sharif wasn't going to let her dictate the kiss. Instead he took the kiss and made it hot, desperate, fierce. He kissed her with a savage hunger that left her trembling in his arms, against his chest.

Lifting her against him he rolled her onto her back and parted her knees with his. She felt him shift over her, the sinewy pressure of his thighs against her own, his shaft rigid against her, pressing against her most delicate flesh. She was ready for him, and yet when he finally entered her it took her breath away. Helplessly she pressed her fingers into his chest, overwhelmed by the size and strength of him. He was bigger, thicker than she'd remembered, and the sensation of silk and heat entering her, opening her, filling her made thought impossible.

Instead she clung to him, arms wrapping around his neck, her mouth turned to his warm scented chest, as he withdraw a little and then thrust again, deeper this time, harder.

Again he withdrew before driving into her, and with each thrust it felt as though he were marking her, branding her, making her his. Indeed it was a taking, a claiming, a ravishment of body and senses.

Sharif filled her, plunging deeply into her, she ground her hips to match each of his thrusts, wanting to satisfy the wildness of her own need, her desire for him insatiable. She wanted as much of him as he'd give her, and she groaned against his chest, craving the power of his sleek body, the hard contours of his back, the lean force of his hips.

She was beginning to lose control and, eyes tightly closed, Jesslyn clung to him, her body tightening convulsively. She felt the tension within her building, the pressure rising swiftly, too swiftly, making her feel as though she'd soon explode.

Sharif's hands covered hers, palm to palm, and as he drove again into her, his fingers laced with hers. And that last thrust pushed her over the edge, sending her shooting into nothingness, just darkness, oblivion.

For an endless moment she felt lost between worlds, no longer attached to her body, her mind spinning away, and then Sharif was kissing her and with one final thrust, he climaxed, his orgasm following right after hers.

Jesslyn felt his body tighten and release and, wrapping her arms around his back, she held him, held him as though she had eternity instead of a night of stolen minutes.

This was, she realized, struggling to catch her breath, the beginning of the end, of the end...of a life as she knew it. No matter what happened now, life as she knew it was changed. Dubai would be different. Dubai was too close to Sarq.

Heart still hammering, body still warm, she held her breath trying to remember this feeling. It was a good feeling. A very good feeling. Being in Sharif's arms wasn't about sex. It was about making things right, making things fit, making her belong.

With Sharif she always felt as if she'd come home.

With Sharif she wasn't that poor little orphaned girl, or that scholarship girl. She wasn't Aunt Maddie's poor niece. With Sharif she was perfect. With Sharif she was whole.

Acid tears filled her eyes, and she closed her eyes, kept them closed, to keep any tears from falling.

Maybe this wasn't such a good idea after all. Maybe making love had just broken her heart all over again.

Suddenly Sharif shifted and the mattress sagged beneath his weight as he moved off her and then climbed from bed. "It's nearly six," he said, standing up and stepping into his trousers.

Opening her eyes, she looked at him. He was reaching for his robe, pulling it over his head and shoulders.

"The staff are already up," he added. "I hear voices down the hall. Mehta will be here soon."

Slowly she sat up, pulled the pale-pink silk coverlet over her to hide her nakedness and only then realized she was shivering. She was cold, freezing cold, her teeth nearly chattering and it was shock that was making her cold, shock that it had ended so abruptly, ended without a kiss or tender word.

But what was he supposed to say? What did she want from him?

And just like that she remembered he'd hired her for the summer. To take care of the children. To teach his heirs.

Eyes gritty, she bit down on her lip and tried to smile, because if he was going to walk out on her she wasn't going to let him see her cry. No more tears, she told herself, not for him, not for her. She got exactly what she wanted—sex. Hot sex. A great big orgasm, and wasn't that fantastic? Wasn't that just what she needed?

Her throat was sealing closed. Her eyes burned like mad but she kept her head up, kept her lips curved.

Smile, she told herself, smile like there's no tomorrow. Smile like you do this kind of thing all the time.

"Are there lessons scheduled for today?" Sharif asked, barely glancing at her as he combed his fingers through his thick dark hair, taming the inky strands.

That's right, Jesslyn thought, chilled to the bone. She wasn't his girlfriend or his lover.

She was the teacher. Hired help. Cheap summer labor.

CHAPTER NINE

"LESSONS?" Jesslyn repeated incredulously, clutching the coverlet to her chest. "On Saturday?"

He shot her a quick look. "What does that mean? You don't work on Saturdays?"

She heard the criticism in his voice and chose to ignore it. "Children benefit from breaks. This is also their summer holiday."

"You know they must get caught up with school."

"And by summer's end, they will be, but what they need most is time to relax, time to play, time to see you and be a family."

"Later today," he answered. "First, lessons with you this morning, and then let them know I'll come during their afternoon tea."

"Oh, lovely, King Fehr. I'll be sure to pass the message on."

He spun on his heel. "What was that?"

She held his gaze, her eyes hot and bright. "You haven't seen the children in nearly a week and you'll make them wait until tea to see you?" She made a soft sound of disgust. What the hell had happened to Sharif, her Sharif, the one she'd dated and practically lived with? Now he was like a stranger again, a king.

That man had been the consummate lover—warm, patient,

considerate—a man who instinctively seemed to know what a woman wanted, felt, and Jesslyn had been so sure he'd be the same kind of parent someday. Warm, patient, loving, kind. But that wasn't who he was at all.

As a father he was far too distracted, which made him too distant with his children. Maybe he wanted to be involved, maybe he even imagined himself involved, but the truth was the girls saw more of their grandmother and nanny than they did of him.

"What has happened to you?" she added roughly, wrapping the coverlet more tightly around her and sliding off the bed. "Where did you go?"

He groaned impatiently. "I don't have time for this."

"No, of course you don't, but then, you're not the Sharif Fehr I knew. That man took care of his friends and family. That man wasn't cold and preoccupied."

"I have a job now."

"You had a job then, and you were successful, and people liked you, people admired you. *I* admired you."

"My people here are happy. My people are content. There is no war, no plague, no devastating disease. The economy is strong. People have jobs. People have lives."

"You don't," she choked. "You have a job, and you work, but you don't have a life. At least, you don't have a life that includes your children."

"I see them."

"Once a week!" Heat rushed through her, warmth burning her cheeks. She was heartsick and disappointed. Disappointed in him. "You see your children for moments in hallways, between meetings and appointments and fights with your mother."

"Why do you think I brought you here? I know they needed help—"

"But I'm not you, and what they need is you." How could he not see that? How could he not understand that he was not just their father but their family? He was all that kept his children from being lost, orphaned like her.

He clenched his jaw. "I'm sorry you don't approve of my parenting skills, but I am trying. I am doing my best. I never saw my parents. And, yes, it was difficult. And, yes, I'd get lonely, but I understood they had important jobs and I understood they cared even if they didn't see me as often as I would have liked."

"Cared?" she repeated. "Is that the same as love?"

"*Jesslyn.*"

"If your children had been sons, would you have been more involved?" She pressed on, a massive lump in her throat. "Would you have had more time for them?"

He took a furious step toward her. "How dare you? How dare you take such liberties with me?"

She pressed her lips together, misery mingling with the brutal disillusionment. "I dare because you came to me a couple of weeks ago and told me your children were in trouble. I dare because you insisted your children needed me, and you needed someone to tell you the truth. So here I stand, telling you the truth." She looked at him levelly. "The girls don't need another paid babysitter or kind stranger. They need you. You, their father, the only parent they still have left."

"And what of my people?" he demanded. "What do I do with the millions who live in this country and look to me for help? What do I do about them? Tell them I can't help them? Tell them I don't have time because I have three daughters who require all my attention instead?"

"Why must you make a joke of it? The girls don't need you all day, but they do need time, each day, every day. If you set some routines, made a point of having dinner with them every night, or some nights, read to them before putting them to bed—"

"Shall I invite my cabinet to story time, too?" he said, mocking her.

She looked at him a long moment before shaking her head in sorrow. "You might be king now, but I liked you better when you were a man."

She wasn't surprised when Sharif walked out without a word or backward glance. After what she'd said, she hadn't expected anything less.

Now with Sharif gone, Jesslyn sat back on her bed and drew the coverlet around her and tried not to think, because thinking at this point wouldn't help. Thinking would just lead to recriminations and she didn't want to feel bad or guilty or anything else.

She had a good life, and when she went back to Sharjah, she'd still have a good life. She had a career she loved and students she adored. Her colleagues weren't just people she worked with, but close friends. She didn't need Sharif or the palace or this complicated life in Sarq. She didn't need his children, either, although she was beginning to think they very much needed her.

In his ensuite bath, Sharif's jaw clenched tight as he stripped his clothes off and stepped into the shower.

What had she thrown at him just before he'd walked out? She liked him better when he was a man?

He bit down harder, knowing she'd hit below the belt on that one. Violently he turned the water on, stepping beneath the spray before it'd even warmed up. It was cold but he didn't shiver. Instead he stood there, icy water pounding down on his head.

Fool, he was such a fool. What had he done, making love to Jesslyn? How could he possibly have thought that would help matters?

No, making love hadn't satisfied him. It'd hurt. Leaving her had hurt. Being with her had hurt.

She felt so good in his arms, so good against his chest where he could almost imagine she was his one true love, Jesslyn, the only one he'd ever loved.

Closing his eyes, he turned around, leaned against the wall, letting the water sluice down.

Zulima had hated him for not loving her better. Zulima had hated him for once calling her Jesslyn while making love. After that she just withdrew from him, completely shutting down and withdrawing to a place he couldn't reach her. But he tried. For years he tried. Yet she wouldn't forgive and he couldn't make it up to her.

And then she died.

Talk about the ultimate punishment—leaving him with a lifetime of guilt.

He felt guilty for ruining his marriage, guilty for depriving his daughters of their mother, guilty for not being a better husband and father.

Turning the water off, Sharif stood in the shower, hearing the water drip.

Who would have thought that an English teacher could level a king?

Finally grabbing a towel, Sharif headed to his room and forced himself to action. After dressing and shaving he headed for his office to start the day.

Sharif's butler was at the door to Sharif's office before Sharif was even there, opening the door for him and turning on the lights.

"Coffee, Your Highness?" the butler asked as Sharif took a seat behind his desk.

Sharif's eyes burned and his body ached as he sat down, but exhaustion wasn't an excuse. It didn't excuse him from work. While he was in Paris and New York problems still arose in Sarq.

"And something to eat. Bread and yogurt. Or some fruit."

"Yes, Your Highness." The butler bowed and disappeared, quietly closing the office door shut behind him.

Almost immediately the door opened again and his mother marched in, the dark silks of her gown swirling with every step.

"You should knock," he said wearily, knowing that his mother fully intended to treat the palace as though it were still hers…forever. That is, if he didn't stop her. And it was time to stop her.

"I want her gone," his mother replied.

"This isn't the time," he answered, not at all prepared to discuss Jesslyn with his mother, much less an hour after leaving Jesslyn's bed.

"Sharif, I'm not in the mood for games."

He smiled. He couldn't help it. It was that or take her head off with his teeth.

His mother wasn't just skating on thin ice, she was jumping on cracked ice. She was going under and she didn't even know. *Yet.*

"I want her—the one you've put in your sisters' room—gone," she added forcefully.

He looked up at her, expression bland. "My sisters have been gone for a long time, and you know others use that room. Just three weeks ago Sheikh al-Buremi's wife slept there."

"How could you bring her here in the first place? She betrayed you. Betrayed all of us by taking that money!"

As if his mother had had no part in the betrayal. As if his mother hadn't baited Jesslyn, tempted her and paid her off.

Sharif tapped a pen on his blotter. Thank God marriage had taught him life-changing lessons like: never show emotion; never show love; never show need. By the second year of marriage Zulima hated all displays of emotion, particularly his. She told him she'd sleep with him but wouldn't kiss him. She'd procreate to produce a child as long as he did it quickly and then rolled off and left.

And is that why he'd made love to Jesslyn and then walked away?

Was he punishing Jesslyn for Zulima's pain, or was he punishing himself?

It'd been hell this morning leaving Jesslyn so quickly and he didn't understand why he left that way. He'd wanted to stay with her but he'd been overwhelmed by his emotion, his passion, his need. It'd been nine years since he'd felt that right with a woman. Nine years since it hadn't been sex but truly making love.

"Sharif." His mother's voice turned shrill.

"I need her," he said simply. "Now if you'll excuse me, I've other things to focus on, things more pressing than worrying about you not wanting an American in the east wing."

"What do you mean, you need her?"

"I mean the children and I need her."

"No, no, absolutely not. Now, listen to me, Sharif. She was wrong for your sisters, wrong for you, and she's definitely wrong for your daughters."

"That's where we disagree," he answered, rising slowly from behind his desk. "She was fantastic for my sisters, she was wonderful with me, and she's perfect for my daughters. Now, it's been a long day, Mother, and I'm not about to start my day by arguing with you. If you were wise, you'd leave, *now*."

"I know you left her room this morning."

Sharif stared his mother down. "How do you get this kind of information out of people, Mother? Do you threaten them or just offer money?"

Two bright spots of color appeared in Reyna's pale cheeks, but she held his gaze. "At least I care about the future of this country! At least I know what is right."

"Do you?" He demanded softly, leaning on his desk, his palms pressed flat to the surface, the muscles in his shoulders flexing, tightening. "Then I'd suggest you take your leave before I have you thrown out."

"Sharif, it is your duty—"

"To provide for you and protect you, yes, I know. But if my brothers knew the truth about you, if they knew you bribe and blackmail and intimidate to get your way, they'd have you on the streets, too."

In the library Jesslyn sat at one of the long tables working with the children. It was late morning with lunch still an hour away and the girls were drooping with fatigue.

"Is our father really home?" Jinan suddenly asked, looking up from her notebook, her dark eyes huge in her face. "Or were you just teasing us?"

Saba and Takia were both looking at Jesslyn now, too, and the longing in their eyes took her breath away. They weren't scared of him, she realized, they were desperate to know him.

Jesslyn swallowed, her heart hurting for the children. "He's promised to have tea with you."

"When is tea?" Takia asked, the tip of her tongue showing through the gaps in her bottom teeth.

Jesslyn had spent the day trying not to think about Sharif and tea. She'd fought to forget last night and the painful way

Sharif had left her this morning. "After lunch, after several more hours studying, and then it'll be tea."

"Four hours," Jinan said.

"Four hours?" Saba groaned, putting her head on the table in despair. "That's so long."

"Forever," Takia agreed.

Jesslyn took in their distressed faces and she wanted to scoop them all into her arms and give them the biggest hug. She loved spending the day with them, it wasn't a chore and it didn't feel like a job. It felt right. The girls needed love and she needed to be needed. It's why she'd become a teacher in the first place.

"How about we do something different for a while?" she suggested, leaning on the table. "What if we do something…fun?"

Jinan shook her head. "We can't have fun. Remember?"

Jesslyn hadn't heard the library door open but suddenly Sharif was there in the doorway. "Why can't you have fun?" he asked, his deep voice surprising everyone so much that the children jumped.

The girls immediately all stood and bowed their head. "Welcome home, Father," they chorused obediently, and yet they were staring at the table, their faces blank.

"Thank you," he answered, walking toward them. "It's good to be home."

He paused, looked at each of them and then at Jesslyn, his expression perplexed. Jesslyn wasn't sure what to do, but it seemed far too awkward to have the children still standing with their heads bowed as if waiting the executioner.

"Girls, perhaps you could sit and show your father what you're working on," she suggested, hoping to sound matter-of-fact and yet horrified that her own heart was beating so fast. Moments ago they'd all been so comfortable, and now tension threatened to slice the room into shreds.

The girls sat down and drew their textbooks back in front of them, but no one spoke or volunteered to go first.

"Jinan," Jesslyn said, "why don't you tell your father about the story you're reading."

Jinan glanced up at Jesslyn, her eyes enormous, expression stricken.

Jesslyn heard Sharif's sigh. He was disappointed. She was, too. She really wanted the children to relax better around him, but he didn't help. He didn't seem to know how to talk to them.

Looking at Sharif she managed a smile. "This morning has been a reading morning. We're all reading short stories and then this afternoon we're going to paint something that could have happened in the story." Pausing, she looked at them, praying they'd jump in, praying they'd try to reach for their father. "Your daughters are excellent readers. All of them."

"I'm not that good." It was Takia and she was worriedly looking up at Sharif, her tongue poking out between the gaps in her bottom baby teeth. "I don't read very good."

Jinan's head jerked up. "She does, too. She's very good for a five-year-old."

Saba nodded and reached out to pat Takia on the back. "That's true. She's a very good five-year-old."

Jesslyn crossed her arms over her chest, hands balling to hide the rush of pride. She loved these girls. Somehow they were becoming her girls.

"Takia, I knew you'd be a good reader," Sharif answered gravely. The girls looked up at him, their foreheads creasing faintly.

"How did you know?" Takia asked.

The corner of his mouth lifted. "Because you loved to chew on books when you were a baby."

Saba giggled. Takia smiled, and Jinan looked at her father with something between bewilderment and wonder.

"Do you remember me as a baby?" Saba asked.

He nodded, and sat down on the edge of the bench not far from Jinan. "Your favorite thing to do was scream."

This elicited more giggles from Saba and Takia while Jinan continued to look at her father from beneath her lashes as though she couldn't decide if it was okay to smile yet.

"And Jinan?" Saba asked, pointing to her big sister. "What about Jinan? What was she like as a baby?"

Sharif looked at his eldest daughter for a long searching moment. "Just like that," he said nodding at her. "So serious. So wise. So determined to do everything perfectly."

"Did she?" Takia glanced back and forth from her sister to her father.

"Yes." He nodded and reached out gently to place his hand on top of her head. "She has always done everything perfectly."

Jinan's head suddenly tipped back and she looked at her father, tears filling her eyes. "I don't do everything perfectly. I don't do anything perfectly." Her small mouth compressed, trying to hide the trembling. "If I did, Mother wouldn't have died and we wouldn't have had to go away to England."

For a moment there was only silence, the deafening kind of silence that follows a lethal blow, and Jesslyn dug her nails into her palms to keep from speaking, to keep from moving forward and filling the awful stillness.

Jaw clamped tight, Sharif let his hand slide from the top of Jinan's head down over her beautiful long, dark hair. "You went to England," he said quietly, "because your mother had gone to school there and it was her dream for you to attend the same school. It wasn't supposed to be a punishment."

"We hate it," Saba said bluntly.

Takia nodded soberly. "We hate it, too," she agreed.

Jesslyn saw Sharif's throat work. He was battling with himself, battling with his emotions. "Maybe you won't go back at the end of summer," he said carefully. "Maybe you can stay here."

"And Miss Heaton can teach us!" Saba cried, turning to grab Jesslyn's hand. "You could stay with us and be our teacher forever."

Jesslyn avoided Sharif's gaze. "I love being with you," she answered, trying to keep things light. "But it's still early in the summer. You might hate me soon—"

"Never." It was Jinan, and her voice was pitched low and fierce. "You're the only good thing that's happened to us since Mother died."

And that, Jesslyn thought holding her breath, said it all.

Queen Reyna rapped on the library door and stepped inside the room. "What's this? No studying? Miss Heaton, I'm surprised at you. I should have thought the children would be working right now."

"I'm giving them the rest of the day off," Sharif said, interrupting her, getting to his feet.

"Oh. Sharif." Reyna took a hasty step backward. "I'm sorry. I didn't realize you were here. Of course you're entitled to visit with the children. I just thought you might have waited until their lunch break—"

"We're going to have lunch now. We'll eat together and then do something fun this afternoon."

"Fun?" Reyna squeaked.

"Fun," Sharif answered, smiling down at the children. "Whatever that happens to be."

After Queen Reyna left, Sharif asked Jesslyn to join them for lunch. During the meal in the formal dining room Jesslyn took in the children's small faces as they talked to their father about what they were studying.

Sharif, she knew, was making a huge effort to ask questions they could answer comfortably. When he didn't seem to know what to say, Saba or Takia leaped in to carry the conversation along, and Jesslyn was touched all over again by the way the children worked together, to help each other, and to even help Sharif.

You couldn't ask for sweeter children, or sadly, more vulnerable children. They'd made some progress in the past two weeks but it wasn't enough. The girls needed stability, security, love, and with ample love they'd thrive. Without it…she shook her head, unwilling to even contemplate a future where the children weren't properly nurtured.

But looking at them now, feeling their excitement, knowing they were thrilled just to be with their father gave her hope. Growing up without a proper family of her own made her appreciate families, made her understand how important it was for children to feel as though they belonged.

"So, what are we going to do later?" Saba asked, ever the brave one.

Sharif surveyed the children and then looked at Jesslyn. He hesitated a moment and then spoke slowly. "I was thinking we haven't used the pool in a long time and maybe you'd enjoy going for a swim."

His words were greeted by silence and then Jinan leaned forward. "In the baby pool?"

He turned to his eldest, his expression every bit as serious as hers. "Do you prefer the baby pool?"

"No, but that's the only pool Jaddah said we can use. She said the other pool is for adults only."

Sharif frowned and appeared to be thinking this over. Then

he stretched out his hands and sighed heavily. "I'm sorry, children, I hate to say this—" he paused and Jesslyn could feel the children's collective sigh of disappointment, "—but your grandmother is wrong."

And then the unthinkable happened.

Jinan giggled. Saba laughed. And Takia cheered.

Sharif looked across the table to Jesslyn and his gaze met hers and held. He was smiling, one of those warm, crooked smiles of his, and it was a smile that reached his eyes, that made the gray irises glow like precious silver. "Thank you," he mouthed.

She nodded, and swallowed around the huge lump filling her throat. It was her pleasure.

CHAPTER TEN

AFTER lunch Jesslyn changed into her practical navy swim suit, which she topped with an equally conservative white terry cloth beach cover up.

Hesitating before the mirror in her room, Jesslyn tugged at the cover-up and found herself wishing she had something more beautiful to wear. It wasn't until she'd arrived here that she saw her life in a different light, saw the spareness and plainness of not just her wardrobe, but her inner life.

Just two weeks here and her world felt full of color and energy and complexity. Just two weeks here and she felt full of life, along with a dazzling range of emotion. Emotion she hadn't felt in nearly ten years.

It wasn't just Sharif, either, that made her feel so much. It was the children. Their need for love and the love they gave her made her feel valuable. Made her want to ensure the children had the best of everything, including the time and attention from their father.

Leaving her room, Jesslyn walked in her flat sandals through the back of the palace to the pool she hadn't even known existed until today.

Waiting outside the pool gate, she peered through the

fanciful wrought iron trying to see all of the pool, which could only be described as a desert extravagance.

The pool had been constructed to look like an island paradise. It had rope bridges and was lushly landscaped with scarlet bougainvillea and palms with a dramatic waterfall as the centerpiece. The towering rock waterfall flowed into one of three enchanting lagoons, and at closer inspection Jesslyn could see that each of the lagoons were really separate pools but with different water features—slides, tunnels and currents. The pool closest appeared quite shallow and even had its own beach where gentle waves lapped onto endless golden sand.

Why hadn't the children begged her to bring them here? This was paradise!

She was still taking it all in when Sharif emerged from the palace. "You could have gone in," he said. "You didn't have to wait out here."

"It looks like Fiji," she laughed, turning to face him. "It's amazing!"

"It was completed just a couple of months ago. I had it built for the children."

She glanced over her shoulder at the waterfall and slides, the little tunnels and coves as though it were a miniature tropical island instead of the backyard of someone's home. "Why haven't the girls told me about it? I would think they'd be here all the time."

Sharif grimaced. "They don't know about it."

"What?"

He nodded, shamefaced. "My mother was very upset about the construction project. She thought it an extravagance, or something one would find in Dubai, not Sarq, so she will only permit the girls to swim in the baby, blow-up pool she keeps for 'special occasions.'"

Jesslyn laughed. She couldn't help it. "A plastic blow-up pool is for special occasions? Wow."

"Mother doesn't believe in spoiling them," he said, opening the gate and leading them into the new tropical oasis.

"It's more than spoiling, Sharif. I'm concerned that she's telling them things that aren't true."

"Such as?" he asked, closing the gate behind her.

She stepped out of her sandals and onto the hot soft sand. "They don't talk to you because they're afraid to—"

"I don't hurt them, Jesslyn. I'd never hurt them."

"But they've been told by Jaddah that they can't bother you."
"What?"

She nodded, grimacing. "The girls told me that your mother has forbidden them from telling you things because you're busy."

"But that's ridiculous. I would want them to talk to me."

"Do they know that though? Have you told them? Made time for them?"

He stared at her, genuinely bemused. "But of course."

"Recently? Since they returned home from school?"

He turned away, walked across the crescent beach, and she followed, the gentle waves from the beach pool lapping at her feet. "Sharif, they're young children and they were gone a long time. They need extra time with you, extra reassurance. Unfortunately, instead of being told how Daddy loves them very much, they're getting the opposite—"

"That Daddy can't be bothered," he concluded, his back to her.

"More or less," she agreed.

"And I thought they hated me," he said half under his breath.

She heard whispers of pain and yet also relief in his voice and, closing the distance between them, Jesslyn put a gentle hand on his back. "You didn't know."

"But I'm their father. I *should* know these things." He turned to face her, his fingers tipping her chin up so that he could look into her eyes. "And I will know these things."

She couldn't hide her smile. "Good."

"It's going to be different from now on. Everything will be different."

"Even better. You have the most lovely children. I absolutely adore them. Speaking of which, where are they? I can't wait to see their reactions when they discover the pool."

He stepped away, looked toward the house, his brow furrowing. "I think their nanny is making them take short naps. She said they needed to wait awhile after eating before swimming."

"But it's already been an hour."

"Probably my mother's involvement," he answered, tossing his beach towel down onto the sand in a spot shaded by a towering palm and then taking a seat on it. "Anything to keep everyone from being happy."

Jesslyn sighed. That was it, wasn't it? Queen Reyna wasn't happy, and so she couldn't bear for anyone else to feel good. And yet what a crime to inflict pain just to keep those around you from feeling peace or pleasure. "Sharif, I'm concerned about her. She seems angrier than I remembered her, and she wasn't happy back then."

"I know. My brothers have noticed it, too. Zayed refuses to have anything to do with her and Khalid's gone to the desert."

"Leaving you to manage her."

Sharif didn't immediately answer. Instead he looked away toward the waterfall dancing over dramatic rocks.

"I know it's not easy, Sharif."

He made a rough sound. "And I don't do it well. The truth is, she makes me so angry, which just makes me feel guiltier. I don't like her here, I don't want her here, but I can't seem to kick her out. From the time I was very small it was drummed into me—protect your mother and sisters, protect and defend them." He looked up at her, his brow furrowed. "I do try, Jesslyn, even though you think I don't. But talking, sharing, all these things that come naturally to you, are very difficult for me."

"Yet you talk to me," she answered, crossing the beach to sit down next to him in the sand.

"You're different."

Puzzled, she tucked a curl behind her ear. "How?"

"It just feels different with you. From the time I met you, I've been able to be myself with you. Not Prince Sharif this, or King Fehr that, but me, the person. The man."

She watched him scoop up a handful of sand, the grains clenched in his fist, delicate rivers of sand sliding between his fingers. "But surely with Zulima—"

"No." He shook his head, opened his hand, let the rest of the sand fall.

Jesslyn leaned forward, arms hugging her knees. "But how could she not adore you? You're smart, very kind, absolutely gorgeous, and you have a body to die for." She blushed, embarrassed she'd said the last part and quickly added, "You've also a wicked sense of humor. How could she not love you?"

His dark head was bent, and she couldn't see his face, just the thick hair at his nape and the sleek muscle that ran along the top of his shoulder. "I made a mistake early in our marriage," he said, his voice low, so low she had to strain to hear him. "Zulima never forgave me for it. Not even on the day she died."

"I can't believe that, Sharif."

He looked up at her, eyes deeply shadowed. "The day she died I was with here in the emergency room. I was holding her hand, telling her we were going to save her, telling her she'd be okay, and she said she didn't want to be saved. She said she'd rather die."

Jesslyn pressed her chest to her knees, struggling to process what he was telling her. "What had you done?"

He made a smothered sound and shook his head.

"Sharif." She touched his arm. "Tell me."

He lifted her hand, turned it over, looked at her palm and her slender fingers and then he kissed her palm before setting it on the sand. "I called her by your name while we were… together."

The kiss on her hand sent darts of red-hot feeling everywhere. "But it was an accident," she said, burying her tingling hand in the sand.

"Of course it was an accident but she knew how I felt about you. She knew I wasn't over you."

Jesslyn looked at his beautiful masculine profile with the black brows, strong nose, firm mouth and hard chin and she didn't think she'd ever loved a face as much as she loved his. And looking at him, she could feel how it'd been with them last night, when they were making love. He was everything she'd ever loved, and she couldn't even explain it, other than it felt right with him, he felt like hers, like the one who'd been made for her.

Impulsively she leaned forward and kissed him, and what was meant to comfort became something else entirely, something blistering and hot.

Clasping her face between his hands, Sharif kissed her with a hunger he didn't even try to disguise. He parted her lips, searched the inside of her mouth with his tongue, tracing the shape of her mouth, the delicate skin inside her lip, but not giving her too much, not giving her enough to satisfy.

Blindly she reached for him, hands settling on his chest, fingers twining in his robe as she struggled to meet her need for more contact, more pleasure.

This was too much, she thought wildly, too fierce, too fiery, too explosive. She felt as if she had a fever and it was consuming her and she needed him to strip her clothes off and drag her into the pool. She needed his body in hers, now, but this need wasn't physical. It came from something deeper, from a part of her that had been so closed, so shut down.

She wanted him, wanted him with a savage thirst and hunger. After trying to live a quiet orderly life all these years she wanted to break free.

His hand slipped down her neck, to the base of her throat where her pulse beat madly, wildly, and then his hand slid lower until he cupped her breast, the pressure of his fingers against her skin excruciating and exquisite. She wrapped her hand around his arm, her fingers digging into the thick corded muscle of his bicep, urging him closer, wanting as much as she could get.

But suddenly he was breaking the kiss off, pulling away and getting to his feet. He took several steps away, faced the waterfall that tumbled into the deepest pool. "Our lives would have been so different if you'd married me," he said roughly, his back to her.

"You wouldn't have had your girls."

He looked over his shoulder at her, expression fierce. "They would have been our girls."

"It wouldn't have worked that way." She swallowed, her heart was hammering so hard it hurt. She needed to tell him about her fertility issues, needed to make him realize he'd done the right thing all those years ago. He might have loved her, but she wasn't the sort of woman a future king could marry.

"The girls could have used a mother like you," he added

bitterly. "Zulima didn't know what to do with the girls once they were born. The children were always with a nanny or nannies, and she'd see them briefly each day, but there were plenty of days where she didn't visit them at all."

"It bothered you."

He exhaled slowly, rubbing his face. "I'd go see the girls at night when they were babies and toddlers. I'd sneak into their rooms and walk with them, carry them outside to look at the moon and stars. I'd tell myself that someday things would be different. Things would be better." His lips twisted darkly. "It never happened."

"That's not true. It's happening now. You're taking the steps you need to take. You're making the necessary changes now."

"But I don't know how to do this. I don't know what I'm doing. I have three children, but I've never really been a father."

"Sharif, it's never too late."

"Never too late," he repeated under his breath before looking at her, creases fanning from his eyes.

He was looking at her as though she was an apparition, a ghost, and it made her uneasy.

"Why did you leave me?" he asked after a long moment. "Will you finally tell me why?"

"We weren't right—"

"We were right." He cut her off ruthlessly. "Everything about us was right. Our relationship was so natural, so easy, so effortless. Why would you just walk away from what we had?"

She closed her eyes, felt the sun pound down on the top of her head. "Your mother never wanted me with you." Just saying the words brought back the awful day his mother had cornered her in her London flat whispering poisonous words that had broken her heart.

Sharif will never marry you. He'll never get our approval

to marry you. No only are you so wrong for him, but you can't have children, can you? And Sharif must have children as Sharif will soon be king.

It'd been crushing to have her injury thrown in her face. She hadn't expected it. She'd never discussed her injury with anyone. Hadn't even known that Sharif's mother knew. "Your mother told me I wasn't an acceptable bride for you."

"And that's why you left me?" Sharif drawled. "You wanted my mother's approval?"

"It wasn't about approval."

"Then what was it?"

She got to her feet and nervously glanced at the palace, knowing the children would arrive any minute. "It's personal. Hard to discuss."

"Come on, Jesslyn, you're a teacher. You can talk about anything."

Not this, she thought, amazed that it could still hurt so much. It'd never been easy to talk about. She loved kids. She'd always wanted kids. Discovering she'd never be a mother had been crushing.

"Would you like some help?" he added, strolling toward her. "Should I tell you what I heard?"

She lifted her chin. "Why not?"

"Why not," he repeated softly, laughing without humor, his features taut, his eyes lit by anger. "Why not indeed." And standing in front of her, he gazed down into her eyes. "My mother said you made a little deal. You'd go away and as a thank-you for your cooperation, you'd leave with some money."

Jesslyn's heart thumped. Was he out of his mind? "You're suggesting she paid me?"

His hands encircled her upper arms, holding her fast before him. "Did she make a deal with you that day?"

"Oh, let me guess who might have told you this," she flashed, trying to pull away but he wouldn't let her escape. "Your *mother?*"

"Just tell me the truth, was there a deal? Did you ever accept money from her?"

It felt like he was punching her, one quick brutal blow after the other. She stared at him through blurred vision. He didn't even look the same—tall, broad-shouldered, raven-haired, towering above her, fierce, furious, frightening.

And even as intimidating as he was now, she knew she'd always loved him. There was no way she could betray him. It went against everything she believed in, everything she held dear.

"No," she whispered through dry lips, her throat parched and her voice even raspier. "I never betrayed you. I never did anything but what was right, what was best." She took a quick breath, a breath that felt like it was on fire. "For you."

"Is that the truth? Look me in the eye and tell me it is the truth."

She flung her head back. "I'm looking you in the eye, King Sharif Fehr, and I am telling you the truth. I am telling you that the conversation your mother and I had that day in my apartment had nothing to do with money and nothing to do with bribes or payoffs or payouts. It had to do with Zulima, your future wife Zulima. Your mother told me that you were engaged, and had been engaged, and that within six months you'd be marrying her."

She yanked free, took a step away, her chin lifted defiantly. "And you did." Then suddenly her lower lip quivered, and all her bravado threatened to disappear. Ruthlessly she bit down into her inner lip to stop the quiver. "You did," she repeated, this time her voice firmer, her emotions once more under control. "So don't you ever talk to me that way again, because the truth is, you never planned to marry me. The truth is your mother had been planning your wedding all along."

A tinkling bell sounded at the large doors, and Mrs. Frishman appeared with the children.

"They're here," she said under her breath as she swiftly, surreptitiously reached up to make sure her eyes were dry.

"We are not finished," he answered quietly.

She was equally furious. "No, we're not."

"I shall speak to you later this evening."

"I can't wait," she seethed.

His eyes narrowed. "I don't appreciate your sarcasm—"

"Then perhaps you'd consider sending me home."

He laughed. "Not a chance. We made a deal. Your bed is made."

"Then you'll know where to find me later, won't you?" she flashed heading for the palace even as the children spied the pool and let out muffled shrieks.

"Jesslyn," he called after her. "Where are you going?"

"I've a few papers to grade," she answered, and then spying the girls she gave them all quick hugs. "You're not going to believe that pool!" she whispered to them. "It's out of this world, and guess what?"

"What, what?" the girls cried.

She tickled their tummies. "He made it for you! Just for you! Go see."

The girls were running through the gates now, laughing as they tumbled onto the sand, their excited voices carrying as Jesslyn disappeared through the palace doors.

She was on the way to her room when Queen Reyna appeared, stepping from the shadows.

"You do know why he's come to you, don't you?" Queen Reyna said, putting a hand on Jesslyn's arm to detain her.

"He's going to marry again. He has to marry again. He needs a son or his brothers will inherit. Now, I don't mind if his brothers inherit. They are my sons, too, after all, but Sharif minds. He minds very much. You must know that he's always wanted to be king. He's done everything he can to be king. Even married someone he didn't love because it was the right thing to do." Her lips curved.

"This is really none of my business, Queen Fehr," Jesslyn said, taking a step back. "If you'll excuse me."

"He's smart, you know. Very smart. He's just using you, using you to get the children whipped into shape so he can bring a new bride home."

Jesslyn wasn't about to bite. She'd known Queen Reyna too long; she knew how the older woman operated. "As I said, it's really none of my business—"

"The bride is already chosen," the queen continued ruthlessly, looking at her from beneath her long black lashes, the same lashes Sharif had inherited. "Or did my son once again forget to tell you that?"

"He told me he might remarry at some point, but there's no bride, there's no one specific in mind—"

"Oh, my, how foolish you are," she said with a little laugh. "You haven't changed. Neither of you. You and Sharif both refuse to deal in reality. He's engaged. The wedding date is set. But of course he won't tell you the truth. He didn't then. Why should he now?"

"It was a pleasure speaking with you, Queen Fehr. I always enjoy these little visits." Jesslyn smiled a blinding smile, battling to hang on to her tattered pride. "Have a nice day."

Reaching her bedroom, Jesslyn closed her door flung herself on her bed, stunned. Exhausted. Numb.

This palace was mad. Everybody, everyone, everything.

She wanted to go back to Sharjah. Needed to go back to Sharjah. Back to her small tidy apartment and her small tidy life. Nothing here was small or tidy. Nothing here let her escape or forget.

Sharif had told her he was thinking about remarrying, she knew that from their conversation during the flight over, but did he already have a new bride in the wings?

Was there one woman already selected and waiting?

She covered her eyes, trying to erase the pictures in her head, pictures of Sharif with another beautiful Arab princess, another gorgeous royal bride with money and beauty and a womb perfect for making healthy babies.

Rolling up, she sat on the side of the bed and stared across the room, past the silk and satin bed hangings, to the sheer silk panels draping the window.

Sharif might be getting married again, but she didn't blame him, couldn't blame him. She also couldn't blame him if he thought the worst of her. She'd never told him why she left. She'd never given him a say, or a choice. She'd taken matters into her own hands and made the decision for him.

No wonder he was angry.

She gripped the bedcovers, thinking she would have been so much wiser—and braver—if she'd just told him she couldn't have children and she knew he needed children.

And apparently from what his mother just said, he still needed that all-important male heir.

A light knock sounded on her door and Mehta appeared. "Teacher Fine," she said breathlessly, "His Highness needs you at the pool. Now."

"Has there been an accident?" Jesslyn asked, scrambling off the bed.

Mehta shrugged helplessly. "His Highness says for you to come now."

Jesslyn practically ran through the palace halls as nightmarish pictures popped into her head. A child missing. A child being pulled unconscious from the pool. Sharif performing CPR.

But instead when she reached the pool the children were playing in the shallow end of the beach pool, with Sharif sitting on the sand close to the water's edge. Mrs. Frishman was nowhere in sight.

She nearly turned around and returned to the palace thinking Sharif was playing games with her, but then Sharif called to her. "Please come here, Jesslyn. I need you."

I need you.

Such powerful heartbreaking words when they came from him.

She joined Sharif on the sand, and he nodded at Takia who was on her tummy floating around, using her arms to get from place to place.

The back of Takia's thighs were shadowed and Jesslyn stared, thinking it odd that the palm fronds above would make such dark reflections on the child's legs when she realized they weren't shadows at all but bruises. My God.

Jesslyn's head jerked up and she stared at Sharif trying to mask her horror.

"Do you see what I see," he said slowly, hardly able to contain the emotion in his voice.

"Yes."

"What the hell is that?"

Biting her lip, Jesslyn leaned forward, seeing more clearly the bruises and ridges on the back of Takia's legs. They were welts, she realized, shock and disgust forming a lump in her throat. "Welts and bruises," she whispered. "She's been spanked."

"That's not a spanking. That's a beating."

CHAPTER ELEVEN

"WOULD you watch my girls?" he asked, his deep voice cracking, his face creased with shock and strain and fury. "I'd like to go speak to Mrs. Frishman."

Jesslyn swallowed. "You think she did this."

"I haven't ever liked her. I should never have let her in this house."

"Go," she said, touching his arm. "The girls are safe with me."

He turned to look at her, really look at her, and Jesslyn caught a glimpse of the anguish in his eyes before his gaze shuttered. "I know they are," he said roughly. "I knew they would be."

He left and she sat down on the soft sand, the water lapping at her feet. She kept looking at Takia's back, and each time she did, shock and disgust made her want to throw up. Takia was absolutely lovely, a little girl who'd immediately stolen Jesslyn's heart, and it was beyond comprehension how anyone could physically punish her, much less hit her so hard as to leave bruises and scars.

Finally, Jesslyn summoned her courage. "Takia, did you fall?" she asked with studied casualness. "I can see some bruises on the back of your legs."

Saba sat up, water streaming from her hair and eyes. "She got punished," she said bluntly.

Takia glanced over her shoulder at Jesslyn, her eyes big, her expression fearful.

"Why did you get punished?" she asked Takia gently.

Takia stopped swimming. Her eyes grew bigger.

"Tell her," Jinan ordered imperiously. "Tell her why."

Takia's forehead wrinkled, and her eyes welled with tears. "I'm bad," she whispered.

"You're not bad," Jesslyn answered firmly, hiding the depth of her shock. What on earth had the child done? Broken something? Stolen something? Lied about something?

"I am bad," Takia whispered, slowly rising from the water to stand before Jesslyn. "I do bad things."

"What?" Jesslyn demanded, lightly holding Takia's wrist and glancing from Takia to Saba to Jinan and back to the five-year-old again. "What do you do that's wrong?"

"I…" Takia ducked her head. "I spoil my bed."

Spoil her bed?

For a moment Jesslyn couldn't understand. And then it hit her. Oh, God. She means she *wets* her bed. A chill went through Jesslyn at the thought of a five-year-old being beaten for wetting her bed.

"Who does this to you?" she asked quietly, her voice nearly breaking with pain.

"Jaddah," Jinan answered matter-of-factly.

Their grandmother? Sharif's mother?

Jesslyn's mind raced. She knew the matriarch was stern, old-school, but to punish a child so severely that welts covered the backs of her thighs? "Not Mrs. Frishman?" Jesslyn persisted.

The girls all shook their heads. "If Takia doesn't stop having accidents she can't go back to England," Saba explained, "and Jaddah says we have to go."

Jesslyn frowned. "Why do you have to go?"

Saba shrugged miserably. "Father's getting married in September."

So even the children had heard about the wedding. Then it must be true. And Sharif hadn't been honest with her. He'd even made love to her despite the fact that he would be married in just months.

Once again she felt shocked—the same shock and denial she'd felt before when Queen Reyna had cornered her in her London flat. She felt cornered now.

Taking a deep breath for calm as well as control, Jesslyn suggested the girls swim for another half hour and then go in, saying she didn't want them to get sunburned.

They nodded obediently and returned to playing and splashing, but Jesslyn couldn't focus, not when her heart was in her throat and her thoughts spun wildly this way and then the other.

The next thirty minutes passed with agonizing slowness. Grandmothers didn't beat their children. Grandmothers didn't threaten young granddaughters. And grandmothers didn't tell their grandchildren their father was getting married before he did.

Mehta was waiting for Jesslyn and the children the moment they returned. "His Highness wants to see you now, Teacher Fine."

"I've the children," Jesslyn answered, "and they're wet and need baths and their hair shampooed."

Mehta nodded and smiled. "I give them their baths. His Highness says I can do that. You go see him."

"No, I want to—"

"Teacher Jesslyn Fine, I have two daughters, two sons. I can give baths. Yes?"

Jesslyn tugged on the belt on her cover-up as Mehta steered the children into their rooms.

She knew Sharif was waiting, but there was no way she could go to his office dressed this way. The cover-up might be fine at a pool but was too short for the palace, much less Sharif's official chambers.

In her room she quickly changed into a straight white skirt with a black-and-white-striped top and scooped her hair into a smooth ponytail low on her neck.

Heading to Sharif's office, she was almost afraid to enter, afraid to tell him what she'd discovered, afraid to confront him about his September nuptials, but she'd do both. She was determined to do both. No more secrets and lies, she vowed. No more hiding the truth.

She rapped firmly on his door. Sharif opened it personally. "Come in," he said, stepping aside.

He was dressed in faded jeans and a casual black polo shirt he'd left untucked. The faded denim fabric clung to the hard outline of his thighs, and his polo shirt, open at the collar, showed the strong tanned column of his throat.

It was the first time she'd seen him in jeans since she'd arrived, and it surprised her and unnerved her more than a little bit. He looked like her Sharif. He looked like the one she'd been so happy, so comfortable, with.

"Mrs. Frishman's gone," he said by way of greeting as Jesslyn entered the room.

"Mrs. Frishman didn't do it."

"I know." He dragged a hand through his dark hair and dropped into one of the armchairs at the opposite end of the room from his desk. "It's my mother."

"So why is Mrs. Frishman gone?"

"She had a responsibility to tell me—or you—what was going on. Instead she covered for my mother."

"How did you find out it was your mother?"

Sharif pressed two fingers to the bridge of his nose. "Mrs. Frishman."

"Did you know Takia had a problem wetting her bed?"

He sat still, his brow furrowed, deep lines etched at his mouth. "I knew Takia had some...accidents...at school. The headmistress wrote to me about it, suggesting Takia would be better off staying home until she outgrew the...behavior." He glanced down at the carpet before lifting his head to look at Jesslyn. "I asked my mother to work with her. My mother said she was."

Jesslyn slowly sat down in one of the chairs opposite his. "You left discipline to your mother?"

He closed his eyes. "I had no idea she'd take her responsibilities so seriously. When we were small, my mother used to hit us with a cane but it never crossed my mind she'd cane my children. Never."

"Oh, Sharif."

His eyes opened, the gray depths dark against the ashen pallor of his face. "This is my fault, too. I blame only myself. I've failed to protect my own children, in their own home."

"You trusted her," she said softly.

"Yes, I did. At least I wanted to. She's my mother, and it's my duty to respect her—" He was cut short by the sound of raised voices in the hall and then a pounding on his office door.

Before Sharif could speak, the door opened and Queen Reyna marched in.

"I guess I can't say she didn't knock," Sharif muttered as he watched Reyna's progress.

"I've just heard about Mrs. Frishman," the queen said, bearing down on them. "She was an excellent nanny and she came with impeccable references—"

"Sit, Mother." Sharif rose and pointed to a chair.

"No, thank you."

"Sit," he said more quietly, his tone harder, less tolerant.

"I will not have you speak to me that way." Queen Reyna cast Jesslyn a disparaging glance. "Furthermore, I will not discuss anything with you until she is gone."

"She's staying," Sharif answered, his voice implacable, like velvet covered steel. "And you're sitting, or I'll have my security detail escort you to the car now."

Reyna sat and this time she did not look at Jesslyn.

"I've seen Takia's bruises," Sharif said without preamble. "I know what you did. You caned her. You've been caning her since she returned home."

"It's just discipline," his mother answered coldly. "Children must be disciplined or they grow up thoughtless, selfish and wild."

Sharif stepped in front of her, stared down at her, his expression bemused. "But you punished her for something she couldn't control."

Her lips tightened. "I was trying to teach her. And yes, I did use the cane on Takia, but it's better to bruise her pride now than to lose her forever." Reyna rose imperiously, smoothing her gown. "Now I'm done here, I won't be interrogated like a common criminal. Sharif, I've packed my things and my driver is out front waiting to take me to the summer house. I won't be back either, at least, not until she's gone," she concluded, nodding at Jesslyn.

Sharif's eyes darkened. "In that case, you won't ever be back."

Queen Reyna glanced from one to the other, smiling a thin hard smile as if she knew something he didn't. "Sharif, it didn't work the first time around. It won't work this time. Your Miss Heaton is cheap, common and completely unsuitable. And yes, we've both already agreed you need a wife, but for God's sake, Sharif, get a proper wife."

An eerie silence descended, and Jesslyn pressed her hands together. She watched Sharif walk to his desk, pull open a drawer and retrieve an envelope. He returned with the envelope, extending it toward his mother.

"I knew it," he said. "I knew all these years you were lying. I knew she would never have taken your money. But I know you'll take mine. Here," he said, thrusting the envelope at her. "A check for a half million dollars. The same amount of money you offered her. A half million. It's yours. Take it. I never want to see you again."

Reyna opened the envelope and looked inside. "What are you doing, Sharif? What is this about?"

"You knew I wanted to marry, Jesslyn," he said, "all those years ago you knew I loved her and I intended to ask her to marry me. But then you went in and whispered little poisonous words, and you ruined everything."

His mother closed the envelope and handed it back to him. "All I did was protect you. I did what any good mother would do. I made sure you didn't throw your future away." She shook the envelope. "Take this back. I can't take your money. It's ridiculous."

"You're right." Sharif took the envelope and, holding it up, tore up the envelope with the check in it in a half-dozen pieces. "I'm not giving you any more money. You're done. You're leaving here and you've gotten all you'll get from me. You can have the summer house. Consider it home."

Reyna stood frozen, her gaze fixed on Sharif's face, the features set in harsh, unforgiving lines. "I wasn't going to let her ruin your life."

"Far better you ruin my life, right?"

"You needed a wife, you needed a male heir and Zulima gave you that heir—"

"He was stillborn, Mother, and Zulima died."

"But at least she could have children." Queen Reyna turned to look at Jesslyn, her gaze almost pitying. "Your dear Miss Heaton, despite all her charms, can't. Her tubes were crushed in that accident in Greece. She's completely infertile." She paused. "Or has she still not told you?"

Jesslyn felt Sharif's gaze as well as his tension. He hated this, all of this, and she didn't blame him. No one liked emotional dramas. But then he looked toward the door and called for his security detail, who had been standing just outside. "Please see Her Highness to her car. I believe her driver is waiting."

Sharif then turned away. He was leaving the room, walking away before he had to watch his mother forced out. Jesslyn couldn't move, though. She felt frozen, rooted to the spot.

"Sharif." Queen Reyna screamed, a piercing heart-rending scream, the sort one might scream on hearing a loved one had died.

Queen Reyna was screaming his name again, but Sharif kept walking.

Jesslyn put her fists to her mouth, horrified, terrified. It couldn't all end like this. He couldn't walk away from his mother like this. Yes, his mother was wrong but this…this…

Reyna was still screaming his name while she was half escorted, half dragged from the room. Jesslyn couldn't bear it. She ran after him, caught Sharif by the arm, held fast. "Please, wait. You don't have to send her away like this."

He tried to shake her off. "She gets what she deserves."

"But I can't bear it. She's wrong. She is. But don't do this. The children can probably hear her. The children have been through enough, too. Please talk to her. Calm her down. Let her leave with some dignity."

Sharif stopped, looked down at her, his expression harsh and unyielding. "But don't you hear her? Don't you hear her lies? She can't stop. Even now, she can't stop. The things she says, the things about you not being able to have children—"

"It's true." She had to cut him off, had to stop him now. "That's true. And it's why I left you. I knew you needed children and I knew I couldn't give them to you."

Sharif's eyes narrowed on her face, but he wasn't listening. He didn't seem to be listening, instead he seemed to be somewhere else, somewhere in his head. "That's what she said to you in the apartment that day. Those were the magic words, weren't they?"

She clung to him tighter, her fingers hanging on to him as though he were a lifeline. "I didn't want you to be the one to tell me to go. I didn't want you to tell me I wasn't enough. I thought it was better for me to leave before it came to that." She exhaled in a soft short gasp. "I thought I was being mature."

"Mature?" he repeated numbly, blinking and refocusing on her.

"I'm sorry. I'm so sorry, Sharif. I didn't want to go, I didn't want to leave you. I loved you so much I felt like it was killing me—"

"Stop," he said hoarsely, turning away.

Jesslyn's hand dropped from his sleeve and she watched him walk away.

"What has she done?" he demanded, his voice low and rough. "What has she done to all of us? What has she done to you? Why does she have such a personal vendetta against you?"

"Because I'm alive," Jesslyn answered softly. She saw Sharif turn toward her and she tried to smile but failed. "I'm here, living, breathing, and your sisters aren't."

Sharif stared at her in disbelief. "No. She can't be so petty."

"She's a mother who lost her only daughters, and in her mind it's not petty. Both her daughters die and I walk away, almost unscathed."

"But you were hurt." He stared at her, his gaze searching her face.

"Yes."

"Yet you came to Aman's funeral."

"No one knew I'd been injured so severely."

He groaned and closed his eyes for a moment as if unable to believe what he was hearing. Then he opened his eyes and extended a hand to her. "Come," he said, "let's go somewhere else. We need to talk, and I don't want to do it here."

They went to her suite as it was far from the palace entrance. Sharif paced the living room floor, and Jesslyn sat on one of the low white couches, a brilliant ruby-hued pillow clutched to her middle.

One of Sharif's butlers appeared with an enormous silver tray laden with coffee, warm fresh bread, small meat pies and pastry snacks, and a smaller plate of dried figs and stuffed apricots. With a bow he placed the tray on the low sofa opposite Jesslyn, then left.

Neither Jesslyn nor Sharif even looked at the food.

Sharif finally stopped pacing. "How do you know you can't have children?"

She stood, and lifting her striped top, and hiking down the waist band of her skirt, she showed him the scar on her abdomen. "Remember this? From the accident?"

He crossed the room, sat down on the edge of the couch and studied the scar on her abdomen. Gently he traced the scar. "You broke your pelvic girdle."

She shivered at the light touch of his finger on her skin. "There ended up being more damage than we realized. I had a lot of bleeding and we discovered belatedly that I'd hurt myself more than we thought. I lost one tube, the other had so much scarring it'd be impossible to conceive, and then the rest wasn't in great shape, either."

He looked up at her, his hands moving to hold her securely by her hips. "But you never told me."

Her heart ached and reaching out she smoothed the deep crease in Sharif's forehead. "I was twenty-two," she answered simply. "I didn't want to believe it was true. So I ignored it, pretended it'd never happened." She gazed down at him, her expression tortured. "Until your mother came to me and reminded me that you needed children and I couldn't give you an heir. Fortunately, she had a solution."

His grip tightened on her hips. "Zulima."

She smoothed the angry furrow between his eyebrows. "I should have come to you myself. I should have told you myself."

"Yes." He tugged her down onto his lap, exhaustion in the deep lines at his mouth and the fine creases at his eyes. "You should have. The only way I know what you need, the only way I know what you want, is if you tell me."

She nodded as she felt his arm curve around her, holding her fast. "I used to hope you'd come after me. I used to pray you'd not forget me."

"And I did." He kissed her on the forehead, and then on her nose and finally her mouth. "I did. And maybe it took nine years, but I wasn't going to give up. I had to find you. Had to see you. Had to bring you to my palace and make you mine."

"I thought you just wanted a teacher," she teased, sliding her arms around his neck.

With one hand he reached up to tug the elastic from her ponytail allowing her dark hair to spill over her shoulders. "A teacher for my children, but a bride for me."

She suddenly wasn't sure what he was saying, and her chest grew hot and tight. "A bride?"

"I need a wife, don't you think?"

She stared into his face, her gaze locked with his. "Sharif, you know—"

"I know," he answered, dropping his head to cover her mouth with his. "I know," he murmured lifting his head long minutes later. "And I don't care. I love you. I want you. I want you to marry me and be my wife, my love, my queen."

He did get married, but it wasn't a September wedding. It was a July wedding at the peak of the summer heat.

Dressing for the ceremony, Jesslyn couldn't believe it was happening, couldn't believe she was the bride this time. A lifetime ago she'd dreamed of being Sharif's wife, and now, after a decade of hurt and heartbreak, her dreams were coming true.

Bathed, massaged with oils, smoothed with scented lotions, Jesslyn was finally dressed, and as she stood before her mirror she couldn't believe the woman she saw.

Even Mehta was awed.

It was the most beautiful gown, Jesslyn thought, reverently touching the white satin embroidered in gold and encrusted with pearls and diamonds. More pearls and diamonds hung from her neck, and a long delicate veil floated down her back, pinned to the small gold crown on her head.

"Teacher Fine is so pretty," Mehta said, hands clasped together. "Now Teacher Fine is a pretty princess."

Jesslyn blushed, blood rushing to her cheeks, and, catching the veil in her hand, she turned away from the mirror, dazzled, overwhelmed.

She did feel like a princess from a fairy tale, and now all she wanted was her prince, her very own Sheikh Fehr.

Less than an hour later Jesslyn stood before Sharif, reciting vows in both English and Arabic. Sharif had incorporated elements from both their faiths in the service, and the ceremony was both intimate and spectacular, beyond anything she could have ever imagined.

Things like this didn't happen to ordinary girls.

Things like this didn't happen to schoolteachers.

The little girls were part of the wedding, too. Jesslyn had insisted they be her junior bridesmaids, and in their beautiful matching pale-gold gowns with darker gold sashes, they looked not just stunning, they looked happy, and they smiled and laughed like little girls should.

After the ceremony Jesslyn caught the children in a hug, not caring that her flowers were smashed, not caring that the hug knocked her crown and veil crooked.

"You're our mother now," Jinan said shyly, touching the pearl and diamond necklace roped around Jesslyn's neck.

"Yes," Jesslyn answered with a kiss.

"Does that mean you're not going to be our teacher anymore?" The little girl persisted.

Sharif overheard and reached out to touch his oldest daughter on the shoulder. "Why do you ask?"

Jinan flushed guiltily. "Because Jaddah said when you got married we'd have to go to boarding school, and we don't want to go back to boarding school—"

"You don't have to go back," he interrupted firmly but kindly. "You can study here at home with a tutor, or perhaps attend one of the small private academies in Sarq that are based on the UK or American curriculum like the American school in Dubai."

Jesslyn lifted her head, looked at Sharif. "Is there an American School in Sarq?"

"No, but there should be something similar. Perhaps that's something I could put you in charge of. Perhaps that's your first job as Sarq's first lady."

"You'd let me start a school?" she asked, trying to contain her delight because she'd loved being a teacher, and education was one of the best ways to touch and improve the world.

"If it was something you'd enjoy doing."

"I'd love it, and I'd love the girls to be our first pupils."

Takia had been listening, and she started jumping up and down. "No more boarding school!"

Jesslyn grinned. "That's right, my darling. No more boarding school. You're home, and you're staying home, right, Sharif?"

He leaned over and kissed each of the girls. "Right."

Later that night, the first night of the rest of their lives, Sharif made love to her as though it was the only night of their lives.

He kissed her and loved her with tenderness and pride and passion. When he took her to the peak of pleasure, he came with her, his body perfectly in tune, and afterward as she lay shuddering in his arms, he held her for hours.

"I didn't even know how lost I was until I found you," he said much later, his deep voice low and husky in the dark. "I was so angry for so many years. I hated myself, hated who I was and what I'd done—"

"Sharif, I can't bear it when you say those things. You are such a good man. You've always been a good man."

"It didn't change my hatred or guilt. But you have. Just having you here, back with me, changes everything."

"Good." She curled closer to him, her cheek resting on his warm chest, her hand on his thigh. "Only happiness now."

"And I can feel happiness now. I knew I loved my daughters, I knew I loved my country, but on the inside I was numb. Dead. And now I know what I was missing. I was missing you."

Jesslyn buried her face against his shoulder, breathing in his warm fragrant skin that smelled of spice and musk and sun. He was beautiful to her, beautiful in a way that was wordless, timeless. It was just him. It was the way he held her and touched her and made her feel.

"I'm so glad you didn't forget me," she whispered, her lips brushing the smooth thick muscle that wrapped from chest to shoulder. "Otherwise by now I might be another man's bride."

Sharif choked on a smothered laugh. "You are all mine, you always were in my heart, *laeela*."

Her smile faded as she thought about Sharif's late wife. "You did care for Zulima, didn't you? You did try to make your marriage work."

He slid his hands through her hair. "I did, and I wanted to be a good husband. I tried my best to be a good husband. It's a terrible thing when a marriage fails, and I never want that to happen again." He lifted her face, looked at her in the dark. "Ours won't fail. I won't let it."

"I won't let it, either," she answered, sliding forward on his body to kiss him. "I love you so much, Sharif."

"I love you more, my queen."

"We're finally together."

He kissed her slowly, parting her lips with his and using his tongue to tease her into shivers of delight. "It's a miracle," he murmured, between kisses that melted her all the way through. "And you are," he said against her mouth, "the greatest miracle of my life."

EPILOGUE

SHARIF was wrong.

The greatest miracle of his life arrived twenty-two months later when Jesslyn gave birth at Sarq's royal hospital.

"The wonders of modern medicine," Jesslyn whispered, cradling the infant against her chest, his small newborn body swaddled in a pale-blue blanket.

"You are a miracle woman," Sharif said, leaning over to kiss her brow, her nose, her lips. "You make miracles look easy."

She laughed softly, exhausted by the long labor and yet euphoric, too. "Easy? Ha!" Six failed in vitro attempts. Six different cycles of drugs, injections, blood draws, egg retrievals…but none of that mattered now. All of that was behind her. They had a beautiful baby, a baby they made together. A baby the doctors said couldn't be made.

Suddenly tears were filling her eyes, tears of joy and gratitude. "Is he really here?" she whispered, stroking his tiny cheek.

"He is."

"And this is real?" she asked, taking the still-unnamed infant prince's hand in hers and examining his tiny fingers and even tinier knuckles.

Sharif leaned over the bed, watching them. "Yes, my darling. This is as real as it gets."

"We have a baby." She shook her head. "A son. A *son*." Abruptly she looked up at Sharif, worry in her eyes. "Do you think the girls will mind a brother?"

Sharif laughed. "Not at all. I think they're going to love a baby brother. Shall I get them?"

"Please. I know they can't wait to meet their new baby."

"Their baby?" Sharif asked, hesitating.

"You know how brothers and sisters are. He'll end up theirs as much as ours." She smiled reassuringly at him. "But that's what we want, isn't it? A family? A real family?"

He stared down at her for an endless moment before cupping her face and kissing her once, twice and again. "I love you, Jesslyn. I owe everything to you. My home, my happiness, my heart. Whatever can I ever do to pay you back?"

She reached up to touch his beautiful firm mouth. "All I want is forever," she said, her voice suddenly husky. "That's not asking for much, is it?"

"Not at all."

She tried to smile. "Just live a long life with me. Be my best friend until we're old."

"I will be with you forever. I will be there when the children go to school and get married and start families of their own. I will be with you here on earth and someday in heaven."

She caught his hand in hers and held it tight. "Do you think that could really happen?"

"Yes."

"How do you know?"

He kissed her fingers. "Miracles are virtually guaranteed with you."

* * * * *

Look for LAST WOLF WATCHING by Rhyannon Byrd—
the exciting conclusion in the
BLOODRUNNERS miniseries
from Silhouette Nocturne.

Follow Michaela and Brody on their fierce journey to find
the truth and face the demons from the past, as they reach
the heart of the battle between the Runners and the rogues.

Here is a sneak preview of book three,
LAST WOLF WATCHING.

Michaela squinted, struggling to see through the impenetrable darkness. Everyone looked toward the Elders, but she knew Brody Carter still watched her. Michaela could feel the power of his gaze. Its heat. Its strength. And something that felt strangely like anger, though he had no reason to have any emotion toward her. Strangers from different worlds, brought together beneath the heavy silver moon on a night made for hell itself. That was their only connection.

The second she finished that thought, she knew it was a lie. But she couldn't deal with it now. Not tonight. Not when her whole world balanced on the edge of destruction.

Willing her backbone to keep her upright, Michaela Doucet focused on the towering blaze of a roaring bonfire that rose from the far side of the clearing, its orange flames burning with maniacal zeal against the inky black curtain of the night. Many of the Lycans had already shifted into their preternatural shapes, their fur-covered bodies standing like monstrous shadows at the edges of the forest as they waited with restless expectancy for her brother.

Her nineteen-year-old brother, Max, had been attacked by a rogue werewolf—a Lycan who preyed upon humans for food. Max had been bitten in the attack, which meant he was no longer human, but a breed of creature that existed between the two worlds of man and beast, much like the Bloodrunners themselves.

The Elders parted, and two hulking shapes emerged from the trees. In their wolf forms, the Lycans stood over seven feet tall, their legs bent at an odd angle as they stalked forward. They each held a thick chain that had been wound around their inside wrists, the twin lengths leading back into the shadows. The Lycans had taken no more than a few steps when they jerked on the chains, and her brother appeared.

Bound like an animal.

Biting at her trembling lower lip, she glanced left, then right, surprised to see that others had joined her. Now the Bloodrunners and their family and friends stood as a united force against the Silvercrest pack, which had yet to accept the fact that something sinister was eating away at its foundation—something that would rip down the protective walls that separated their world from the humans'. It occurred to Michaela that loyalties were being announced tonight—a separation made between those who would stand with the Runners in their fight against the rogues and those who blindly supported the pack's refusal to face reality. But all she could focus on was her brother. Max looked so hurt…so terrified.

"Leave him alone," she screamed, her soft-soled, black satin slip-ons struggling for purchase in the damp earth as she rushed toward Max, only to find herself lifted off the ground when a hard, heavily muscled arm clamped around her waist from behind, pulling her clear off her feet. "Damn it, let me down!" she snarled, unable to take her eyes off her brother as the golden-eyed Lycan kicked him.

Mindless with heartache and rage, Michaela clawed at the arm holding her, kicking her heels against whatever part of her captor's legs she could reach. "Stop it," a deep, husky voice grunted in her ear. "You're not helping him by losing it. I give you my word he'll survive the ceremony, but you have to keep it together."

"Nooooo!" she screamed, too hysterical to listen to reason. "You're monsters! All of you! Look what you've done to him! How dare you! *How dare you!*"

The arm tightened with a powerful flex of muscle, cinching her waist. Her breath sucked in on a sharp, wailing gasp.

"Shut up before you get both yourself and your brother killed. I will *not* let that happen. Do you understand me?" her captor growled, shaking her so hard that her teeth clicked together. "Do you understand me, Doucet?"

"Damn it," she cried, stricken as she watched one of the guards grab Max by his hair. Around them Lycans huffed and growled as they watched the spectacle, while others outright howled for the show to begin.

"That's enough!" the voice seethed in her ear. "They'll tear you apart before you even reach him, and I'll be damned if I'm going to stand here and watch you die."

Suddenly, through the haze of fear and agony and outrage in her mind, she finally recognized who'd caught her. *Brody.*

He held her in his arms, her body locked against his powerful form, her back to the burning heat of his chest. A low, keening sound of anguish tore through her, and her head dropped forward as hoarse sobs of pain ripped from her throat. "Let me go. I have to help him. *Please*," she begged brokenly, knowing only that she needed to get to Max. "Let me go, Brody."

He muttered something against her hair, his breath warm against her scalp, and Michaela could have sworn it was a single word…. But she must have heard wrong. She was too upset. Too furious. Too terrified. She must be out of her mind. Because it sounded as if he'd quietly snarled the word *never*.

HARLEQUIN *Presents*

He's successful, powerful—and extremely sexy....
He also happens to be her boss! Used to getting his
own way, he'll demand what he wants from her—
in the boardroom and the bedroom....

Watch the sparks fly as these couples
work together—and play together!

IN BED WITH
THE BOSS

Don't miss any of the stories in April's collection!

MISTRESS IN PRIVATE
by JULIE COHEN

IN BED WITH HER ITALIAN BOSS
by KATE HARDY

MY TALL DARK GREEK BOSS
by ANNA CLEARY

HOUSEKEEPER TO
THE MILLIONAIRE
by LUCY MONROE

Available April 8
wherever books are sold.

HARLEQUIN *Presents*~

Don't forget Harlequin Presents EXTRA now brings you a powerful new collection every month featuring four books!

Be sure not to miss any of the titles in
In the Greek Tycoon's Bed,
available May 13:

THE GREEK'S FORBIDDEN BRIDE
by Cathy Williams

THE GREEK TYCOON'S UNEXPECTED WIFE
by Annie West

THE GREEK TYCOON'S VIRGIN MISTRESS
by Chantelle Shaw

THE GIANNAKIS BRIDE
by Catherine Spencer

I ♥ HARLEQUIN Presents

BROUGHT TO YOU BY FANS OF
HARLEQUIN PRESENTS.

We are its editors and authors
and biggest fans—and we'd
love to hear from YOU!

Subscribe today to our online blog at
www.iheartpresents.com

REQUEST YOUR FREE BOOKS!

2 FREE NOVELS PLUS 2 FREE GIFTS!

GUARANTEED
PASSION · SEDUCTION

YES! Please send me 2 FREE Harlequin Presents® novels and my 2 FREE gifts (gifts are worth about $10). After receiving them, if I don't wish to receive any more books, I can return the shipping statement marked "cancel". If I don't cancel, I will receive 6 brand-new novels every month and be billed just $4.05 per book in the U.S. or $4.74 per book in Canada, plus 25¢ shipping and handling per book and applicable taxes, if any*. That's a savings of close to 15% off the cover price! I understand that accepting the 2 free books and gifts places me under no obligation to buy anything. I can always return a shipment and cancel at any time. Even if I never buy another book, the two free books and gifts are mine to keep forever.

106 HDN ERRW   306 HDN ERRL

Name	(PLEASE PRINT)	
Address		Apt. #
City	State/Prov.	Zip/Postal Code

Signature (if under 18, a parent or guardian must sign)

Mail to the Harlequin Reader Service:
IN U.S.A.: P.O. Box 1867, Buffalo, NY 14240-1867
IN CANADA: P.O. Box 609, Fort Erie, Ontario L2A 5X3

Not valid to current subscribers of Harlequin Presents books.

Want to try two free books from another line?
Call 1-800-873-8635 or visit www.morefreebooks.com.

* Terms and prices subject to change without notice. N.Y. residents add applicable sales tax. Canadian residents will be charged applicable provincial taxes and GST. This offer is limited to one order per household. All orders subject to approval. Credit or debit balances in a customer's account(s) may be offset by any other outstanding balance owed by or to the customer. Please allow 4 to 6 weeks for delivery. Offer available while quantities last.

Your Privacy: Harlequin Books is committed to protecting your privacy. Our Privacy Policy is available online at www.eHarlequin.com or upon request from the Reader Service. From time to time we make our lists of customers available to reputable third parties who may have a product or service of interest to you. If you would prefer we not share your name and address, please check here. ☐

HP08